Beloved Benjamin
Is Waiting

Beloved Benjamin
Is Waiting

by JEAN E. KARL

E. P. DUTTON ≈ NEW YORK

Library of Congress Cataloging in Publication Data

Karl. Jean E.   Beloved Benjamin is waiting.

SUMMARY: Hounded by a gang of kids after her mother's disappearance leaves her on her own, Lucinda hides in the abandoned caretaker's house in the local cemetery where she makes contact with intelligent beings from another galaxy.

[1. Family problems—Fiction.   2. Life on other planets—Fiction]   I. Title.
PZ7.K139Be   [Fic]   77-25286   ISBN: 0-525-26372-1

Published in the United States by E. P. Dutton, a Division of Sequoia-Elsevier Publishing Company, Inc., New York
Published simultaneously in Canada by Clarke, Irwin & Company Limited, Toronto and Vancouver

Editor: Ann Durell   Designer: Meri Shardin
Printed in the U.S.A.   First Edition
10 9 8 7 6 5 4 3 2 1

≈ ≈ ≈ ≈ ≈ ≈ ≈ ≈ ≈ ≈ ≈ ≈ ≈ ≈ ≈ ≈ ≈ **For Mary**

≈ ≈ ≈ ≈ ≈ ≈ ≈ ≈ ≈ ≈ ≈ ≈ ≈ ≈ ≈ ≈ ≈ ≈ ≈Before

"BUT WHAT will you do, Lu?"

Lucinda didn't know. Hadn't thought about it.

"You can't stay here alone. It was okay when there were two of us and they were fighting. But it's not okay for one. You could get hurt."

"I'll go outside then—into the yard or something."

"That's silly. You can't stand around in the yard at night. And what if it should rain? Or snow? Besides, there are those guys, Dean's gang. They're still mad because when he got caught, he told on Biggs. What do you think those guys would do if they saw you in the yard at night?"

"I can hide under the front porch." She giggled, knowing he hated the spiders and things there as much as she did.

≈ 1

"Look, Lucinda, be serious. You've got to decide before I go. I won't feel right otherwise."

"Well, you can't stay home. Not after all the work to get you into that school!" It was silly of him to worry so, just because she might not be safe when Mama and Pa had a fight! She could take care of herself, although sometimes she wished she was going to a fancy boarding school, too.

Mama didn't like it, of course. She'd miss the work Joel did around the house. And she didn't see that it was dangerous for Joel to stay. Dean's old crowd wouldn't leave him alone, not now.

But Mama refused to think about things like that. Just like she never cared what she or Pa did to anyone when they had a fight. Joel was right. It wouldn't be safe to stay. But where could she go?

"Would Kate take you in?"

"Once in a while, I guess. But their apartment is so small."

"Yeah, it would be taking advantage. But what are you going to do?"

Her gaze strayed to the cemetery across the street. She had never been in. The fence with its iron bars and electric current kept everyone out, except the people the men at the gates let in. And that never included kids from the neighborhood. But she'd always liked the way the cemetery looked, liked the openness and the space of it. She wondered what it might be like to hide out there. It was impossible, of course. But she looked at it just the same, wishing for a way in, just once. And then she began to wonder. Was it really so impossible? There was that little gate . . . over by the old house. . . .

"Hey, Joel, what about the cemetery?"

"I told you, be serious! Nobody can get in there."

"I am serious. Remember that little gate, the little wooden one? By that old house nobody lives in. You know. The little wooden gate in the metal fence, the one that looks as if it was put in so somebody could shove deliveries through without bothering the people in the house or having to go into the cemetery."

"But it's so small, just big enough to shove a box of groceries in. And besides, it's probably locked."

"It isn't. Don't you remember? We looked once. It latches, but it doesn't lock anymore. Unless somebody fixed it. And only somebody small could get through, so they probably don't think it's worth fixing, if they even know it's broken. Remember, we thought that I might be small enough to get in, but we never dared try. At night, though, who would see?"

Joel looked at her as if she were crazy. Yet something in his face said the idea wasn't bad.

"You're nuts, Lu. Even if you could get in, you wouldn't want to stay in a cemetery!"

"Why not?" She shrugged. "It's safe in there. Safer than here."

"That's for sure." His face was thoughtful. "Do you really think you could get in?"

"Let's try and see."

A few minutes later the problem was solved. Lucinda did fit through the gate—just. There were plenty of bushes inside for cover. And Joel thought that if she needed more shelter, the old house or some shed inside might do, as long as she was careful.

"Okay, Lu, now you know what to do. If it gets bad—if they start throwing things or hitting—just sneak out and get over here quick. And don't let anyone see you go in. You don't want to get caught."

"I know. I know. I can make it," she said as they turned to go home. "There aren't many people on this street at night. You don't have to worry."

Actually, the thought of what she would have to do scared her a little. But she didn't want Joel to know. Besides, if she had to do it, she could. You could always do what you absolutely had to do. So there was no point in getting upset in advance.

"Well, I will worry, and not just about that. You have to be careful, Lu. You hear? It's not just Mama and Pa. It's all those guys Dean hung around with. Stay away from them, you hear. You never know what they'll do. And don't let anyone know when you're home alone. Promise?"

"Oh, don't be such a squash, Joel. Those guys haven't bothered us much so far. Maybe it's only Dean they're after. Besides, you know I'll be careful."

"Listen, just remember that those guys are smart. Smart enough to let Dean get caught while they're still free, except for Biggs. And that's Dean's fault. They've got an eye on us, but they're not going to do anything that will get them in trouble. At least not something they can't get out of. But they're watching. So don't be alone, if you can help it. Stay with Kate or Pamela or someone like that after school. Try to play it safe. Promise?"

"Okay, okay. But don't worry. I can take care of myself. I'm not going to get caught. And I'm sure not going to advertise when I'm alone. I know better than that. I have some sense."

Joel smiled. "Yeah, I guess you do. And I suppose I do worry too much. You're a pretty practical kid, Lucinda."

She laughed, and they ran into the house.

≈ 1

THEY were at it again. Lucinda moved stealthily along the wall, creeping through a shadow to the door. Quietly, hardly daring to breathe, she turned the knob, pulled the door gently, pressing down on the knob to keep the dry hinges from squeaking, and as soon as the crack was wide enough, slipped through. Then noiselessly she closed the door behind her. She was out. She sighed with relief. Her knees felt shaky, and she thought she might have to sit down on the front steps. But that didn't make sense. She had a place to go, and she'd better get there.

Why did her parents fight? Lucinda had never figured it out, and Joel had never known either. Cherry always said it was because they were unhappy. But lots of people were unhappy and didn't fight, didn't throw things, didn't lash out at anything and everyone around.

She remembered the time Cherry had gotten her arm broken, just because she was in the way when their father threw a kitchen chair. All four of the kids had been in the kitchen hiding that night, but after that they'd found better places to go—sometimes inside, more often outside. But a year ago Cherry had left for college and her job as a mother's helper. And last spring Dean had gone to the training school, sent there by the judge because of the drugs. Then she and Joel had been left alone.

They had hidden inside the house when they needed to all summer. It had been okay inside for two. They could hide more easily than four, and yet they could protect each other if necessary. But now that Joel was gone, it didn't seem like a good idea to stay there alone. You never knew what might happen. So she was off to the cemetery. It hadn't seemed like quite so strange a place to go when she and Joel had decided on it. But now she wondered. Could she really do it? What would it be like? Would it be scary? And what were the chances of being caught? There was no help for it, though.

Things had been quiet at home since Joel left. Her father had been away mostly. Sometimes he had to go places for a job, she thought. But that wasn't the only reason he stayed away. Though where he went she didn't know. And why he came home, when he did come, she didn't know either.

Most of the time when he was there she stayed away from him as much as possible. He had an awful temper, and it was best just to try to be invisible. Even her mother did that. Lately, though, her mother had been gone, too. She'd been working someplace as a waitress. In a bar, Lucinda thought. That's what they were fighting about now. About her mother not being home very much anymore. Her father didn't like it. Mama was supposed to be there when he came home. But Mama said he never gave her enough money, so she had to work.

Neither of them had paid much attention to Lucinda lately. It was almost as if she weren't there, as if she really were invisible. And her mother sometimes forgot that Joel was gone. She called for him as if he should be there. It was all hard to understand.

When the fight began right after dinner, Lucinda thought it might not be a bad one. Sometimes they weren't. But then it was. The two of them were all over the house, her father chasing her mother and her mother grabbing things to throw at him. So Lucinda had known it was time to go.

And now here she was, about to sneak into the cemetery! A tingling feeling in her spine, half fear and half anticipation, made her move faster than she usually did. She cautioned herself—slowed down, not wanting to call attention to her movements. It was after sunset, but still light enough for someone to see her.

She turned the corner and walked down the street as if she were headed for some distant spot, pretending she didn't have a place nearby to go. At the same time, she was aware of everything going on around her. There was no one else on the street. None of Dean's gang there, thank goodness, although she really hadn't seen much of them since Joel left. Maybe because she'd been careful to keep out of their way.

Almost too soon she was at the little wooden gate. With a quick glance, she looked around once more. Two of the houses across the street were empty, sold and going to be remodeled. Just shells of houses now until the work was done. Then there was a vacant lot. The houses beyond that were probably too far away for anyone in them to notice her. Besides, the people there were the kind who never saw kids, unless they made too much noise. It was really other kids she had to watch out for most. They were the ones who would see her and ask questions.

She heard a shout, but it came from around the corner. Quickly, before anyone could come, she lifted the latch, got down, and slid through, almost on her back, swinging under the low bar at the top of the opening. In seconds she was deep inside a thick clump of bushes, where she hoped no one could see her. She was pretty sure, especially in the growing dark, that no one would.

The gate, she remembered then, was closed but not latched. Someone might notice. She'd have to go out and fasten it. But not until later. And after this she'd have to remember to do it when she came in. If she came another time.

She settled quietly on the ground, her arms around

her knees. It was nice here. Except for the brief moment she had been inside before Joel left, she had never done more than imagine what it might be like to be inside the fence. The leaves were dry with September, and some were falling. But even so, there was a green, rich feeling to the place.

With a questioning glance, she looked toward the old house. Did anyone live there now? She and Joel had decided no one did. Peering through the bars of the fence, they had never seen anyone who looked as if he might live there. Not that she knew what someone who lived in a cemetery ought to look like. She giggled to herself, then looked at the house more closely, trying to make out some of the details in the near dark.

There were no curtains on the windows. Of course, there were almost no curtains at her house either. But that was different. People who lived in a house like this would have them. It was a funny old place with lots of fancy carving that looked like lace around the small porch and up on the edge of the roof. What for? Just to look nice, she supposed. It seemed odd that anyone would have taken the trouble. But then the house was old. And people long ago had been different.

Grandma had been different. Lu had never thought about that before. Grandma had liked nice things around her. The memory of her grandmother brought a sudden catch to Lucinda's throat. She didn't think about Grandma often. The whole family had come here to live with her just after Lucinda was born, because her father had been gone for a long time then and her mother had worked in an office. Grandma and Cherry, who was eight when they moved, had taken care of the house and Dean and Joel and Lucinda.

But it had been hard, Cherry had said. Because Grandma hadn't been very well. She was nice, though. Lucinda could still remember the long stories she had told them, when she said she "just had to sit down." Some had been real and true, and some not. But they were all good.

Dean had never listened much, though. As far back as Lucinda could remember, he had always been restless, had always been out. She wondered briefly about him, where exactly he was. But actually he didn't concern her now.

When she felt settled enough to be restless herself, she moved from under the bush, shivering slightly in the wind. Why hadn't she brought a sweater? She'd be really cold if she stayed all night. And she supposed it wouldn't be a good idea to go home until morning. It would be a nuisance to creep back only to find the fighting still going on.

Well then, she needed some place where she would be out of the wind. There was less wind under the center of the bushes, but the bare ground there was damp, damper than the grass.

The house? She looked at it again. The bushes pressed to within a few feet of it. She could get almost to it without being in the open. Was there a night watchman who came around? She hadn't seen one yet. But there probably was one. She drew back into the bushes in a flurry of indecision. It wasn't too cold. No point in taking a chance when it wasn't necessary. If she got caught, there would be no end of trouble. It was better to be a little cold and be safe.

She settled back with her head against a tall tree, a little out from the leaf-moldy earth right under the bushes. She was a bit in the open, but really well protected, especially in the dark. And she could watch to see if anyone came. No one was likely to see her, she felt, since no one expected her to be there. People, she knew, saw what they expected to see.

It was later, much later. She pulled her head up with a jerk. She must have been asleep. Had she made a noise? Surely not. It was really chilly now, sitting there on the ground. Was that what had awakened her? No, there was a noise! She listened intently. It sounded like a car or some kind of machine. Smaller than a car, but moving. Not a motorcycle. Had someone gone past and seen her?

As a light appeared out of the distance, she crept quietly into the heart of a bush. A man was just coming—sitting on a motor scooter; that's what the noise was. He came down the drive that went in back of the house and then around and away. She was sure that his eyes were scanning the area, but he didn't stop.

Now she knew that there was at least one man in the place at night. How often would he come by? Had she missed an earlier visit while she slept, or did he come only once a night? Or maybe twice? Did it matter, if he didn't look any more carefully than he had? Not right away it didn't. He was gone, and she felt quite sure he would not be back soon. But some other time he might look more carefully. Should she have a better place to hide? Should she check the house? There would be time now, with the man just having gone past. And she had to find some place to go in case it rained. Joel had said that.

With the sound of the motor scooter already far in the distance, she crept on her hands and knees to the house. She went to the back door first, because from there she could not be seen from the street. After slipping cautiously up the steps, she reached for the doorknob. To her surprise, the door was unlocked. She had not really expected that. Should she go in? Yes, she had to know what was there, in case sometime she needed to hide inside.

Opening the door as carefully as she had the door at home and then closing it with equal care, she moved into what was a very dark place. A half moon had come up outside, but it did little good inside because the bushes around the windows were so tall. She could see just enough to know that the room she was in had been used for storage. There were old tools, a few broken tombstones, or at least that's what they seemed to be, and other things she couldn't identify in the dark.

Picking her way carefully in the scattered light, she

moved from one room to the next. The room at the back, the one she had come into first, had the most stuff in it. As if whoever carried the things in hadn't wanted to go any farther than necessary. There were four rooms on the first floor, and two were almost empty. It was clear that this house was not a working part of the cemetery anymore. It was the grave-yard—she giggled at the thought—for unwanted things. This idea made her bold. It wasn't scary in there. Just peculiar.

In the front room there was a narrow staircase that led to an upper floor. She knew she shouldn't climb old stairs, that they could give way with her. But somehow she couldn't resist trying them. She was small and light, and she would be careful. Feeling each step ahead of her, testing it before she put her weight on it, and holding tight to what she was sure was a very dusty banister, she made her way up, making a mental note to take some of the old rags she had seen in the second room downstairs and run them over the whole banister, so that no one could see her hand marks.

At the top of the stairs, it was darker than anywhere below. She felt, rather than saw, a hall and perhaps a door ahead. Moving cautiously, she thought of getting down on her hands and knees, but there was no telling what was on the floor. Better to test each step with her foot instead. Her hands felt ahead, too, seeking for something solid. And at last they found it. A door that swung, creaking on its hinges, at her touch.

As the door opened, her eyes, used to the dark hall, were surprised by moonlight, brighter here than below because there was not so much shrubbery to block it. The room had once been a bedroom, and it still was, in a way. A funny old bed with a high metal headboard and footboard stood by one wall, and a dresser stood on the opposite wall. In between there were two windows, on the back wall of the house, that let in the light. There was no chair, no rug on the floor. But there were remnants of curtains at the windows, pulled back and hanging in rags.

Lucinda was so amazed she could hardly believe what she saw. Why would anyone leave anything in an empty house? But maybe nobody had remembered that this furniture was here. She wondered if there were other rooms, and if they, too, had furniture. Pushing the door all the way open so that some of the moonlight seeped into the hall, she ventured out of the room and back past the stairs. There was another room at the front. As she pushed the door open, she saw a room almost as dark as the hall, because the moon was on the other side. Light from the street, however, showed that it was empty. She turned around and went back to the first room, the one with the bed.

Looking up, she saw that the ceiling was flat in the middle, but slanted down on the sides. The room was up under the roof then. She stepped over to the bed and touched it. The mattress felt firm and dry. Evidently the roof did not leak. There was an old sheet over the mattress, but no bedclothes. She pulled the sheet back a little and realized that the mattress underneath was old, but not too dirty. The sheet had protected it.

She moved to the dresser at the other side of the room, pulling out each drawer and feeling cautiously inside. They were all empty. How sad for a bed and a dresser to be left so alone. She giggled again at herself, then yawned. It must be really late. Later than she had ever been up before, except on the nights when her parents had a fight. Which this was, she realized with a start. It hadn't seemed like that kind of a night. Coming here had been an adventure, a kind of exploring.

Would she dare tell Kate tomorrow? On the way to school they always told each other all the things they had done the night before. Kate knew all about hiding from fights. But this didn't seem like something you could tell Kate. She wouldn't understand how really unscary it was. Then, too, Kate just might tell her mother, which would not be a good idea.

Lucinda yawned again. The bed looked comfortable. She wondered if it was. Stepping over to it, she felt it for a second time, pulled back the dirty sheet, and sat down. It wasn't bad. A little saggy. And it smelled funny. But it was almost as good as the one she had at home. She stretched out on it, full length. Even without a pillow, it felt good.

The next thing she knew there was a light in her face. Startled, she sat up quickly, the old spring protesting in a squeak. There was no one around. Thank goodness! The light was simply the day, ready to begin. She had slept the night out in the old house.

Realizing that she had to get out of the cemetery before anyone was around, she got up quickly and pulled the sheet back on the bed. There were tracks all over the floor where she'd walked. Those had to go. Hurrying downstairs, she found the remains of an old broom among the tools. With this she hastily tried to at least eliminate her footsteps, although if anyone looked carefully they would have to know that someone had been in the house. Looking around again by the pale dawn light, she could tell that no one came into the house very often. Nevertheless, she swept the banister, too, and then left the broom near the back door. She might need it again.

After creeping down the back steps and through the bushes, she made her way to the gate. She had forgotten to go back and latch it last night. Well, no one seemed to have noticed. Next time she'd be more careful. When she was sure no one was near, she slipped out and ran home.

The house was quiet as she came in. The fight was over. One of the kitchen chairs had a broken leg. And a pile of broken glass lay in a corner. A bit of blood had dripped from there to the sink. That was all the evidence there was of the night before. She listened, then crept to look in the bedrooms. No one was home. Which was not like the other times. Generally one of them was still there after a fight. Sometimes both.

She hurried to her room, which she had once

shared with Cherry. Looking in the mirror above the dresser, she realized just how dirty the old house, and maybe the ground under the bushes, had been. What a mess! She went to the bathroom, stripped off her clothes, and took a cold bath. They never had any hot water. Only her father knew how to work the heater, and he almost never turned it on. He said they couldn't afford it.

The next problem was finding something to wear. Luckily she did have a clean blouse and a pair of jeans that weren't too bad. She slipped into them with relief. If she had to go to the cemetery often, she'd have to have special clothes to wear there, so she wouldn't get her regular clothes so dirty. Laundry had become a problem. Her mother seldom thought of it. Lucinda had long ago decided she needed more clothes so she didn't have to wash so often. Enough so she could fill a machine at the laundromat when her mother remembered to give her some money. When Joel had been there, it had been easier.

Joel! Had he left some old jeans and stuff, things he'd outgrown that maybe she could wear if she had to? She hurried into his room, and in the mess in his drawer, she found both jeans and ragged tee shirts. Fine for the dirt of the old house. She took them back to her room and slipped them into a drawer. Now all she had to do was find an old sweater and maybe a blanket and some sheets to take, and she'd be all set, at least until the cold weather came.

It seemed almost too easy. Though maybe because

everything was working so well, she wouldn't have to go again. Things often went that way, she'd found. Of course, there was always the problem of getting in and out of the old house unseen. But even that didn't worry her much. The street where the gate was wasn't used by through traffic. And the guards in the cemetery didn't seem to check often. Only that man on the motor scooter.

You'd think with all the crazy kids in the neighborhood, the cemetery would need more protection. How could the cemetery people be so sure no one would get in? She wished she knew more about how things were run there. That would make it even safer.

≈ 2

"DID YOU get your arithmetic done?" Kate asked.

"Oh, sure," said Lucinda absently, wondering if she should bring some clean rags to the old house next time she went. They might be good for wiping up some of the dust.

"You did! I don't believe it. What's wrong with you this morning? You're not listening to me. Did your folks have a fight last night? Mine had company, so I couldn't get anything done."

"I heard you. I did do my homework. I woke up early, and I didn't have anything else to do." That much was true. She'd been ready for school so early, even after scrounging around for something to eat, she'd had plenty of time. "It wasn't hard."

"But it took a lot of time," Kate grumbled. "I don't

know why they have to give us so much. It's fun being in sixth, though, isn't it? The oldest ones in the school. It makes you feel as if you're getting somewhere."

Lucinda nodded. It was fun. "Some schools change at fifth now, or even fourth," she said.

"I like it better this way. You appreciate being the oldest more when you're eleven."

"Yeah, maybe," said Lucinda.

"The only trouble is the homework. And then we'll have to do that dumb history paper, too, the one they always do in sixth. I suppose old Pritchard'll be telling us soon: 'Now, people, in the sixth grade, we have a very special project. . . .' "

Lucinda laughed. Kate sounded just like Ms. Pritchard, but she couldn't remember about any project. "What history . . . ?"

"Oh, you know, that local history project. Where you're supposed to dig up some piece of local history and write a paper on it."

"Oh, yeah!" Lucinda did remember. Joel had done it. A lot of kids, she thought, just copied what somebody else had done some other year, changing it a little, maybe. But Joel had tried to find out about an old newspaper that had once been published just for their part of the city. He'd found some copies of it at the library. The paper he wrote had been really interesting.

"I remember now. I guess you're right. She'll tell us pretty soon. But there's no point in worrying about it till it happens. Besides, maybe she's tired of reading the same old papers every year. Maybe she'll want us to do something new."

"Don't be crazy! She's a history teacher; she can't do something new." They both laughed.

"Hey, there's the bell. Let's go."

That day at school went better than most. It was the first time since school started that Lucinda had had her homework done. There really was never as much of it as Kate thought. And it didn't take long to do, but Lu hadn't been in the mood for it this year. The house seemed empty without Joel, and she had felt too restless to settle down to anything.

She did try to keep the house straight, as she and Joel and Cherry had done for years. Not that she liked doing it, but she hated a mess more. She'd been doing a lot of cooking, too. It was hard to cook for yourself when you didn't know much about it and didn't have much to cook with. And the things her mother bought and had in the house generally didn't go together very well. Sometimes she knew what to do with what she found, and sometimes she didn't.

She'd gotten a cookbook from the library, to get ideas. But all the recipes called for things she never had—at least not all together. What did you do with lettuce and peanut butter and an orange? That was all she'd been able to find one day. She'd eaten the peanut butter on the lettuce, using lettuce leaves like bread in a sandwich. And then she'd eaten the orange. It hadn't been bad. But it was a strange kind of meal.

When Lucinda got home that day, there still was no one there, even though it was late. She'd gone to Kate's after school. But then Kate's mother had said Kate had to go shopping for a new pair of jeans. They had invited Lucinda along, but she'd decided not to go. It would make her want a new pair herself all the more. She really needed them. But her mother had to be in just the right mood before she could ask.

Since she had nothing else to do at home, she sat down and did her homework. It had been kind of fun to have it all done that day. It made things a lot easier. Wouldn't the teachers be surprised though. Two days in a row! Still, her grades had always been pretty good.

It was quite late when she went out to the kitchen to look for something to eat. The hot lunches they had at school didn't taste good, generally, but they did stick with you. There wasn't much around home, as usual. Some bread and a little salami. An apple. She made a sandwich and ate the apple.

She was getting ready for bed when she heard her mother come in, and a few minutes later her father. As soon as she heard their voices, shouting at each other, and the sound of things breaking, she knew she was in trouble. And when she heard her mother lock herself in the bathroom and her father throw himself against the door, trying to knock it down, she knew she had to get out of there.

Two nights in a row! All the patterns were changing. Generally there was a week or two between big fights. She'd counted on that, hoping her mother would get into a better mood, one where she'd consider buying her a new pair of jeans.

"What's the matter with you?" her father shouted, still slamming himself against the bathroom door. "No, I do not need a steady job. And yes, you will do as I say."

"Get out of here," her mother screamed.

"Since when are you telling me what to do? This may have been your mother's house, but it's mine now." Something cracked in the door.

Whew, Lucinda thought. Keep that up and the Winskis all the way across the burned-out house next door would get an earful. They might even call the police. And what that would mean for her parents—or for her—she didn't care to think. She changed quickly into her outdoor clothes, grabbed the things she had put together to take along, and slipped out of the house. No point in taking a chance when there was a perfectly good place to go. But two nights in a row! That was pressing her luck at the cemetery.

Nevertheless, she was through the gate and into the old house almost before she knew it. Nothing had changed since the day before. It was dark, because the moon was not yet up, but she could tell that things were just as she had left them. Still, it was best to be careful.

She picked her way quietly up the stairs, pulled the old sheet off the bed, and slipped on the worn but clean sheets she had brought and the old holey blanket. Then into a pair of Joel's pajamas. It was almost like home. If only she had a pillow.

She was ready to climb into bed when another thought struck her—did the old place have a bathroom? It must have. Houses long ago didn't, she knew. But this one wasn't that old. There wasn't one upstairs. But downstairs maybe? She slipped downstairs, and after stubbing her toes a couple of times and almost tripping over a statue on the floor, she found a door in the kitchen that she hadn't opened the day before. And sure enough, there was a bathroom. Amazingly, the water ran. She didn't dare drink it, because she couldn't see well enough in the dark to tell if it was clean or not. It might be rusty from sitting in old pipes. But even so, she could hardly believe her good fortune. A person could really live here.

As she felt her way back through the kitchen, trying to stay near the wall and keep low, out of sight of the windows, just in case, she stubbed her toe on the statue again—an old gravestone, she supposed, set up near the wall. She felt it, and it seemed to be the statue of a person, a child maybe, but she couldn't really tell. She didn't remember having seen it the morning before, but in her rush she had probably overlooked it. She rather hoped it was a child. It would seem like company in the house.

What would Kate and Pamela and the other kids at school say if they knew where she was? she wondered suddenly. They'd be scared to come, she thought. Maybe think she was crazy. That might be why the cemetery guards didn't seem too worried about people coming in.

But she wasn't afraid. Why not? she wondered. She guessed it must be because this was so much better than home. Now *that* was something to be afraid of. At least on nights like this. She felt her way back to the stairs, climbed up, dashed down the hall, and crawled into bed.

She went to sleep easily, but awoke in the middle of the night. Had she heard someone? For a moment she froze in fear. What had awakened her? There were no footsteps; there was no light. The room was very dark, and a soft rain pattered against the window. Maybe that was it—the rain. But no, there it was again! A sound. A soft humming sound. She listened. It was an electricity sound that seemed to come from the wall.

But that was impossible. There might be electric wires in the wall, but surely the electricity had been turned off, even if the water hadn't. Maybe it was rats, or mice, or roaches. Or maybe even bees. Yet it didn't sound like any of those. And it wasn't the scooter. Now that she was really awake, for some reason the sound didn't frighten her. It wasn't a people sound. It was just part of the overall place. She yawned and went back to sleep.

She woke again as it got light. The rain was still falling, but softer than in the night. She got dressed and pulled the sheet that belonged to the house over her own sheets. No one would know how many sheets had been on the bed, surely. And hers were old enough to have been there a long, long time. She slipped the clothes she had brought and the blanket into a dresser drawer. They might be more suspect if someone found them, but she had to take that chance. She couldn't keep carrying them back and forth.

She stepped downstairs, got the broom, and again swept the dust to cover her tracks. On the way out she stopped and looked at the statue she had kicked the night before. It was metal of some sort, iron maybe, painted black, and it was of a boy. The arms were broken off, which was why it was in the house, she supposed. At the bottom, the pedestal on which it stood said:

BELOVED BENJAMIN
BENJAMIN PIERCE FINE
BORN APRIL 5, 1882—DIED MAY 9, 1889
AGED 7 YEARS, 1 MONTH, 4 DAYS
OUR LIGHT, OUR LIFE, OUR JOY: NOW WITH GOD

Stooping to read the inscription, she noticed that she had moved the statue a little when she kicked it the night before. She gently moved it back to just the place it had been, uncovering a pipe that came just to the top of the floor. It must have had to do with gas or something in the kitchen. The thought of gas made her shudder. She moved the statue back over the pipe and swept the dust around to cover up the fact that the statue had been moved a little. Then she left.

She picked her way carefully out of the cemetery so she did not leave tracks anyone would recognize in the damp ground. At home, she found that the quarrel was over. Her parents were both there, asleep. She didn't dare take a bath for fear the sound of the water running would wake them, but she did get herself as clean as possible at the kitchen sink. She didn't want to go to school dirty. People might ask questions.

Once she was dressed for school, she went into Joel's room. The thought had occurred to her that he might have left other things she could wear. Even some of Dean's things might do. She spent an hour sorting through the leftover clothes she found in the room. Then she went back to her own room because she remembered a few things Cherry had left.

When she finished, she had two piles of clothing—three, really. One was a pile of things she could actually wear to school. Another was a pile of things she could wear to and from the old house so she wouldn't have to get her school things dirty. And finally, there was a small pile of things she would take to the house the next time she went and leave for emergencies. With the last group of clothes, she put some other things she thought might be useful—a flashlight, some rags, some towels, and so on.

Her life, she decided, was shaping up; it even seemed exciting, full of mystery and adventure. There was always the chance she might get caught at the cemetery, of course. But she didn't think it was very likely. Instead, the cemetery seemed like a safe and lovely secret.

Again she wondered, as she pulled her books together, how she could find out more about the cemetery. If she knew how it was run, what the men who worked there did and how many there were around, she'd know what was safe and what wasn't. But how could she find out without making people suspicious?

As if her mind had been working on the problem without her knowing it, suddenly the answer was there. Of course there was a way: the local history project! The cemetery would be a perfect topic. She could find out a whole lot without giving anything away. It might even be sort of interesting. The dates on Benjamin's statue proved the place was old. And there must be people buried there who had lived nearby. So it had to be a part of local history. And probably no one had ever done a paper about it. So she would just have to do some research.

But where would there be information? At the library? Perhaps. And maybe one of the men who worked at the cemetery would talk to her. She could go to the main gate, the one on the other side from her house, and see. If she had a letter from Ms. Pritchard, or maybe even from Mrs. Jones, the principal, it might work.

Almost forgetting the need to be quiet, she danced out the front door. How soon, she wondered, would Ms. Pritchard assign the project? It would be awful if she did decide to do something different this year. But she couldn't. She just couldn't. She was a history teacher, and history was a kind of stay-put subject.

≈ 3

AGAIN that day, there was no one home when Lucinda got back from school. She was late because she'd
gone to Pamela's, and Pamela lived in the other direction from school. No one, not even her mother, came
home that night. Someone had bought a few eggs and
some frozen vegetables, though. It must have been
her mother.

Cherry had always said that it wasn't that their
mother didn't like them or didn't think about them, it
was just that she had so many problems, she had to
keep running to stay ahead of them and didn't have
time for much else. That hadn't made much sense to
Lucinda until lately. Now she could see that in a way
her mother did seem to care. She seemed to miss
Joel. And there was almost never a time when there
wasn't something for Lucinda to eat.

Thinking about her own problems that night, Lucinda wondered again about the cemetery. Ms. Pritchard hadn't mentioned the local history project, so she couldn't get a letter for the gateman yet. But there would be no harm in trying the library. She could say she needed to know about the cemetery for a school assignment, even if it was a little ahead of time. The library must have kids come in every year asking about things for that paper, so it wouldn't seem odd.

The next afternoon, Friday, she went to the library right from school. Kate thought she was crazy. "Go to the library on a Friday?" she said. Lucinda just laughed.

She liked books, especially books that told you how to do things. Once she had done a plant experiment from a book, had grown some seeds just like the book said. But the jars they were growing in had all gone to pieces in one big quarrel. Joel had told her she was foolish to cry. But she had cried, and she had never tried to do anything like that again. She still read the books, though, sometimes.

At the library, Ms. Clipp knew all about the usual assignment.

"You're the first to come in this year," she said. "I didn't remember that that project came so early in the fall. Ms. Pritchard must be changing her schedule. I do wish those teachers would let us know so we could be prepared."

"I'm just getting started early," Lucinda said. "The paper isn't due for a long time."

Ms. Clipp looked as if she approved.

"I don't remember anyone doing the cemetery," she said. "It's a good thing you are starting early. There won't be anything in the children's room. But let me take you into the adult local history section. There are some old books there that might help."

By the end of the afternoon, they had found very little. Only a few people had written about the cemetery when they wrote about the old days in their part of the city. Lucinda had learned when the cemetery was first started and by whom—the people in a downtown church. She had read a list of famous people buried there, but none of the names sounded familiar. And she had seen a map of how it was laid out and an article about who had done the planning. The map was a help. It let her see exactly where the house was and what else was near. That was the only thing that was really useful. But she took everything down on a piece of notebook paper. She would, of course, really write the paper, as well as get information for herself.

"Come in again," Ms. Clipp said as Lucinda left. "I'll take you into the microfilm room, and you can go through some of the newspapers from back in the 1870s and 1880s. I'm sure there will be good bits of information for you there. Maybe in the papers for Memorial Day for those years."

Lucinda nodded. She would come back. She'd need the information for the paper, although it didn't sound too useful for herself. She might find out about Beloved Benjamin, though. That would be nice.

When she got home, Cherry was there. She lived

with a family in another part of town, a long way away. She had a scholarship to a college over there, and when she had graduated from high school, one of the teachers had helped her get this job where she mostly helped take care of the kids. And she got time off to go to classes. It was what she wanted to do, although she had hated leaving Joel and Lucinda.

"I can't do anything for you here, though," she had said. "And maybe there I can. At least after I graduate, I can get a good job and help you."

It was because of Cherry that Joel had gotten the scholarship to the boarding school. The father in the family she worked for had helped.

Lucinda was glad to see Cherry now. She never knew when she would come home. There was no phone in the house anymore, so Cherry couldn't call.

"How are you doing?" Cherry asked.

"Okay," said Lucinda, not wanting Cherry to know too much.

"Have they been fighting?"

"Two nights in a row this week," Lucinda said reluctantly.

Cherry looked upset. "What did you do?"

"Joel and I worked it out before he left," Lucinda said. She didn't want to tell about the cemetery. It might sound a lot worse than it was. But then she changed her mind. If someone should catch her there, it would be best to have the guards or the police or whoever it was call Cherry instead of her mother. So she explained what she had done.

Cherry looked more and more upset.

"Weren't you scared?" she asked. "How could you go in there and sleep? In the cemetery!"

"It's just a house," Lucinda said. "Somebody lived there all the time once. It's the safest place to go."

"It's just the idea of it. I always used to wonder how anybody could ever have lived there. It isn't right for you to have to do that. I ought to tell Mrs. Rice, see what she says. She worries about you, too, Lucinda, feels you shouldn't be here. Yet Mama was so upset about Joel's leaving, it didn't seem right to take you away, too. And besides, I don't know where you could go. There are foster homes, but we've never had anything to do with that kind of thing. Some agency does it, I guess, some part of the city government. The trouble is, you never know what people in the government will do. That's what Mr. Rice says. And I guess he's right."

The idea of a foster home horrified Lucinda. There'd been a girl in her room at school once who was in a foster home. She'd been moved four different times, to four different families. All of them mean to her, she said. And she was a tough girl, a lot tougher than Lucinda. Sally had said she never saw her real family anymore either. And that would be worse than anything, Lucinda decided. Not to see Cherry or Joel.

"Mama would make a fuss if I left," she said quickly. "And I don't mind the cemetery. It's kind of an adventure. It's so peaceful there. I can't explain it. I feel as if nothing bad can happen in that house."

"Well, just be sure you have my phone number

with you in case you get into trouble. Now come on. I've made you a decent supper. How long has it been since you've had one? I thought I'd have to leave before you came."

"If I'd known you were coming, I'd have been home earlier. I just went to the library, but I didn't have to go today."

"There was no way you could have known. Anyway, I got a few things in. There wasn't much to eat here."

"We never run all the way out. She always sees that there's something."

Cherry sighed. "I've got to leave soon. The Rices are going out tonight. I wish I could take you with me, even just for the weekend. Maybe sometime I can. I don't think Mrs. Rice would mind. As I said, she really does worry about you."

That was a new idea. Lucinda had only been all the way across town once or twice. It would be like going to a new place altogether, and it might be fun.

"I'm okay," Lucinda said. "Don't worry about me."

Cherry ruffled her hair. "You need trimming. Get the scissors, and I'll do it for you before I go."

Lucinda got the scissors from the place where she kept them hidden, and they talked about Joel and about other things until Cherry had to leave.

"Be careful, Lucinda," she said, and gave her a kiss. "I'll be trying to work out something for you. Be good."

"I will," Lucinda promised, and then turned away so Cherry wouldn't see her tears. She had never understood why having someone around made you feel so much more alone when they left.

No one came home at all for the whole weekend. It was the first time that that had happened. Lucinda spent most of Saturday at Kate's and even had supper there Saturday night. She liked Kate's mother and dad and her two brothers. Kate's family was fun.

On Sunday, after spending so much time at Kate's on Saturday, Lucinda didn't feel she could go back again. Someone might begin to ask questions, and she wouldn't know what to say. She was tired of being home alone, though, and it made her mad that her mother didn't come back. It wasn't fair. She felt like throwing things herself, but decided she might do a little cleaning up instead. Everything would at least look neater. But it wouldn't be the way it had been when her grandmother was alive. Then it had felt like a home. It didn't now.

When she finished the house, there was still part of the day left. She could go to Pamela's, but it was a long way. And she was careful about how far she went alone, even if she hadn't seen any of Dean's old friends around. Besides, Pamela's family generally went to visit relatives on Sunday. There were other kids closer, but none she was sure would be home.

With nothing else to do, she read a library book and then did her homework. In one way it made her feel good to do it. But in another it worried her. If she suddenly seemed to know too much, some of the kids might resent it. It would call attention to her, and that's just what she did not want to have happen. It wouldn't pay to have too many people notice her, for a lot of reasons. There were even some kids in her class who were related to some of Dean's old gang. It would be best if they, especially, didn't become too aware of her. Well, she'd just have to watch out.

It was after school on Monday that she finally had to cope with one of Dean's old friends. After she'd been avoiding them so well! She and Kate were walking home when Tom Williams came out of nowhere.

"Hey, Lu," he called.

She started to run, but Kate held her back.

"Don't do that, dummy," she said. "You want him to think there's some reason you shouldn't talk to him?"

"I don't want to talk to him!"

"Well, don't show it," Kate whispered. "No matter what you know about him, remember he's Rosella's brother and she's in our class. You can't get away."

"What do you hear from Dean?" Tom yelled.

"Nothing," Lucinda said firmly. "Nothing at all."

"Where's Joel? Haven't seen him around," Tom went on. "Got a couple of friends I thought he might like to meet."

"Gone away," said Lucinda.

"When'll he be back?"

"Not for a long time."

"Too bad. We had plans for him. See you around, Lu."

He sauntered off, and Kate turned on Lucinda.

"You shouldn't have told him that!"

But she didn't need to say it. Lucinda knew herself just what she had done. She could have killed herself. If it really mattered to them, and she thought it did, before nighttime that whole gang would know that she was the only kid left in her house.

"Now they'll know you're alone, or . . ." Kate stopped in embarrassment, not wanting to tell all she knew about what went on at Lucinda's house.

But Lucinda wasn't embarrassed. She was worried. "What will I do, Kate? What do you think they'll do?"

Kate couldn't answer, and they walked along in silence.

Fortunately Lucinda's mother was home that night, though with little to say. Lucinda told her about Cherry's visit on Friday, but her mother only scowled. She seemed hardly to be listening.

Lucinda wished she could mention her worries about being alone, but she had a feeling that nothing would break through to her mother.

For the rest of the week, her mother just sat. She was always home, for a change. Didn't seem to be working at all. But she didn't do anything else either. Lucinda did the cooking for them both, although her mother didn't eat much. A couple of times her mother roused enough to give Lucinda money to buy things at the store, but those were the only times she said anything.

Her father came home twice, but he and her mother did not even say hello. Both times he took some things from their bedroom, some clothes, Lucinda thought, and left.

Several times during the week Lucinda almost said something about Dean's old gang, but then she didn't. What could she say? What was she afraid of, really? Besides, she hadn't seen Tom Williams or any of the others since Monday. She hurried home from school every day, though, because it seemed safer. It gave no one a chance to ask more questions. Kate understood, and so did Pamela; and once Kate came home with her to play awhile. But it was sort of awkward, with Lucinda's mother just sitting there. So Kate didn't come again.

To make matters worse, it rained most of the week. That helped when it came to not seeing people on the street. But she thought it might be part of her mother's trouble. Her mother hated rain.

By the weekend Lucinda had decided that being in the house with her mother the way she was now was worse than being in the house alone. So Saturday afternoon she went to Kate's, and Pamela came over. They had a good time playing Monopoly. Lucinda went home long before dark, though. No point in taking chances.

Sunday was a dull day. Again she did her homework because she had nothing else to do. She even read ahead in a couple of her schoolbooks because she hadn't been to the library in over a week and had read everything she had at home twice. How could her life be so empty all of a sudden? Yet what could happen to make things better? She thought about Cherry's suggestion of a foster home and decided that would be worse. Why go from troubles you sort of understood to troubles that would be all different and maybe even more difficult to handle. She couldn't forget Sally.

Then on Sunday night when she was getting ready for bed, her mother came into the room, talking almost like her old self.

"Lucy, do you think you could manage alone here for a week or so?" she asked. "I really do have to go away. After that I hope I can be home more than I have been lately."

"Sure," said Lucinda. It seemed that whether her mother was there or not, she pretty much managed alone. Except . . . except for the gang. Should she tell her mother about them? She almost did, then decided not to. Her mother would surely remember that they were the ones who had gotten Dean in trouble. Yet even so, she would probably think that Lucinda's fears were foolish. So Lu only nodded, though inside, the thought of a week alone began to upset her for all kinds of reasons.

"It may be as much as ten days," her mother warned.

"That's okay," Lucinda said; but it wasn't. Ten days was too much. There was no chance that people wouldn't notice. It left too much time for things to happen. Bad things of all kinds. The Winskis might notice and report it to whoever you told things like that in the city. Or Tom Williams . . . Well, what would he and that gang do? She had no idea.

"Will Pa come home?" she asked.

"No, he's gone for good," her mother said shortly. Her face closed up, and Lucinda knew better than to ask any more questions about that.

"Will there be enough here to eat?" she asked, trying to think and plan in spite of her fears.

"I'll give you some money," her mother said. "Keep the doors locked, whether you're here or not. And don't do anything foolish. Not that I think you would. How I managed to have so many straight-backed kids, I'll never know." She shook her head. "I suppose I should be glad. But it does get to you. Well, anyway, Lucy, do the best you can. I've got to go. Tomorrow, I think. So don't expect me when you get home from school."

Lucinda wondered if she should call Cherry. But what could Cherry do? A foster home was Cherry's only answer so far. And that was no answer at all. She'd have to bluff it through alone somehow. To quiet her panic, she tried to think of the good side of it. After all, she was going to be here alone and would have some money. She could buy the things she liked to eat and not just have the things her mother got.

The main problems would be the Winskis and those friends of Dean's. And would any of them really do anything if they found out? Was she worrying for nothing? After all, as Kate had said, Rosella was Tom Williams' sister, and she never paid much attention to Lucinda. She even smiled at Lucinda sometimes. Maybe there wouldn't be a problem.

Lu drifted off to sleep in a haze of vague worry,

only to have her dreams take her to dark and night-marish places. It was almost a relief when morning came. Somehow it was easier to face real things and to be up and around.

Before she went to school, her mother gave her thirty dollars. "Take care of it, Lucy. Don't spend it all at once. If I'm not back in ten days, you'd better call Cherry. You have her phone number, don't you? But don't tell her I'm gone before then. Promise me you won't. There's no reason why you should call her. She doesn't need to know I'm gone. And don't worry about Pa. He won't be around. I've seen to that."

Lucinda ran off to school worried and upset. Where was her mother going and why? Why shouldn't she tell Cherry? What were her mother's reasons? And where had her father gone? She might even welcome him home now. It was all so confusing.

On top of the bad morning at home, a lot of bad things happened in school. She kept having the feeling that everyone knew she was going to be alone for a whole week, maybe more. It was all just imagination. Nobody could know, not yet. But she felt uncomfortable anyway.

Worse than that, every single teacher took that day to comment in some way on how well Lucinda was doing. She cringed the first time. But by late in the day she just looked icy and felt cold inside. It was nice to have people say good things, but she didn't need the attention—not today, not this week. She had been trying so hard to just sink into the class and be forgotten. When a teacher asked a question, even when she knew the answer, she never raised her hand. But on the written work, on the homework and on tests and stuff, it hadn't seemed necessary to hide what she knew.

It was the comments, not the fact that she was alone, that made her conspicuous, she finally decided, that made her feel she was being watched. What mattered was being noticed. She had seen Rosella look at her strangely, and she didn't think that was imagination.

She hoped Kate would walk her all the way home; but before she could ask, one of the teachers stopped her in the hall, wanting to know about Joel. Kate vanished out the door, thinking, Lucinda supposed, that the conversation might take a while. Kate's mother liked her to come right home. And that left Lucinda alone.

Unfortunately, when she left the building, it turned out she wasn't alone after all. Rosella and Janice and Carmella and even a couple of boys were waiting for her. Kate was way down the block already. Lucinda said "Hi" to the group, tried to ignore them, and set off at a deliberate pace down the street.

The group followed her. Most of them were kids she didn't know well, some of them in her room and some not.

"Lucinda, will you help me with my homework?" Rosella singsonged.

"Lucinda, will you write a book report for me?" Janice called. And the whole bunch laughed.

The taunts went on and on, and then Rosella had a

stone, tossing it from hand to hand, pretending to throw it forward when Lucinda took a moment to look back.

Lucinda finally had to run. Hardly knowing what she was doing, she dashed home as if her life depended on it. Too many things had happened. She couldn't think clearly. Couldn't plan. Just had to get away. It must have been the fear that made her able to run so fast, because she was soon way ahead of the others, though she could tell they were still following. She reached her house well before them, opened the door, threw herself in, and locked the door behind her. A stone hit the front door as she sank to the floor, exhausted.

She could hear the others outside then, shouting and laughing. Another stone banged against the door. If only they didn't begin to break windows!

"What do you kids think you're doing?" It was Mrs. Winski. Lucinda had never believed she would be glad to hear that voice, but now she sighed in relief.

The kids shouted something back, but then ran off; and Lucinda put her hands over her face and cried. What was she going to do? What would happen if people found out that her mother was gone? What would those kids do next? Were they mad just because of what happened in school today, or was Tom Williams behind this? Was the gang still mad at Dean? Would they beat her up if they caught her tomorrow? It could happen.

The kids following her—it couldn't be just because

of what the teacher had done. Other kids got good grades. It had to be because she was Dean's sister. And somehow they know something about her mother. If they didn't know she had gone away, they at least knew she wasn't doing much for Lucinda, that they could get away with tormenting her.

Suddenly she was furious with the whole lot of them. Who did they think they were, running after her like that? She was glad Dean had told on Biggs. Those kids—they all had more money than she did, regular families, too, and lived in better houses. Did they think that made them better, that they could get away with anything they wanted to do? She'd show them.

Nevertheless, she sat on the floor a long time, not really knowing what to do. What were her choices? She could call Cherry. But her mother had made her promise not to do that. And besides, that could mean a foster home. She could make it seem as if she were not alone in the house, turn on all the lights, pull down the shades, and maybe even pretend she was having a conversation with someone, changing her voice. She could leave earlier than usual for school, get there before anyone else, and maybe find new ways to come home, leave at different times, so the kids would never be quite sure where to look for her. It was only for a week. Then her mother would be home. And maybe in a good mood, a listening mood, and she'd help after that.

Feeling better, she got up, began to turn on the

lights, even though it was still light outside, and pull down the shades so no one could see in. Once she had that done, she felt better.

There wasn't much in the house for supper, since she hadn't been able to get to the store, but she wasn't very hungry.

It was almost dark when Lucinda heard a noise in the rubble of the burned-out house next door. The Winskis lived beyond on that side, but she knew it wasn't the Winskis. It sounded like boys' voices.

Lucinda crept to her bedroom window and looked out, peeping under the pulled-down shade. It was Tom Williams and a friend. They were sitting with their backs against one of the burned-out walls next door, looking at her house. Tom Williams had a stick in his hand.

"But all the lights are on, Tom."

"Sure, and all the shades are down. She's alone in there all right. Maybe even listening to us, right now. Which is fine. The more scared she is, the better. Now's our chance to get even for Biggs. To get back at that dumb Dean."

Their voices were low, but Lucinda could hear them quite easily.

"You're sure he's gone?"

"I said so, didn't I. And Mrs. Gratz, too. Only Lucinda home. Which makes it just perfect. We get her and the house, too. Of course, we can't use the house forever, but it'll give us the hideout we need while we need it. And no one will ever know."

"The kid won't tell?"

"Not when we get through with her."

"How do you know the Gratzes are gone?"

"I keep my eyes open. And I've got friends who do, too. You know that. Sometimes it pays off, like now. We've got a score to settle here. Actually, I've just been waiting. I had a feeling Mrs. Gratz would blow sometime. Dean always said she was weird. And the old man is almost never around anyway."

Lucinda was scared. But she was mad, too. What right did Dean have to say that about their mother? Besides, she wasn't gone for good, only a week.

"Hey, let's get on with it. Break a window, that's the best way." It was Tom Williams again.

"Are you crazy?" the other kid said. "I thought you had this all planned. Don't you know how nosy those Winskis are. We can't do it on this side of the house."

"I guess you're right. I didn't think of that. It would probably be better if we broke a lock on a door or something. Wouldn't make so much noise. Let's try the back door."

Lucinda crept to the back of the house. Was the back door locked? Yes, she was sure it was.

They were there now, rattling it quietly.

"Have to jimmy this lock," Tom Williams was saying. "Look, you stay here. So the kid will know someone's around, won't try to run for help. Though if I know her, she's too scared to do anything anyway. I'll go get Sarkan. He's great at locks. Maybe bring some of the other guys, too. Wait here. I won't be long."

≈ **47**

He raced off. Lucinda could hear his feet. And the other kid, after rattling the door a few times, seemed to settle down out there.

What should she do now? She couldn't fight them, though she wanted to. Dirty sneaks. It wouldn't do any good to tell the police. That would only get her in trouble. No, she had to get away. And the only place to go was the cemetery. There was nothing else to do, unless she wanted to tell someone about her mother. After what those boys had said, that was the last thing she intended to do.

She had money, the money her mother had given her. And she already had most of the things she'd need at the cemetery put together. What else should she take? Her schoolbooks and her library books. What food she could find. A few dishes and kitchen things. Hastily she gathered up all the things she could think of and put them in two shopping bags. Her actions were mechanical. Her mind was on the problems ahead. She'd be staying at the cemetery for a week. Could she do it? She still didn't know much about what went on there, about how many men worked there. But no matter how risky the cemetery might be, home was now really dangerous. There was no choice.

She had it all together: her school stuff, the clothes, the flashlight, towels, food in an old metal can of Joel's. It was really lucky she hadn't gotten to the store today. She couldn't have carried a lot of food. This way she still had the money.

Ready to leave, she looked around the house once more. What was she forgetting? Nothing she could think of. What would happen to the house? No way of telling. But there was nothing she could do to save it; she could only save herself.

With the skill of years of practice, she slipped out the front door noiselessly. Even her bundles didn't keep her from being so quiet she could hardly hear herself.

Luckily it had grown dark, and there was no moon. It was cloudy and even a bit foggy. She kept low and close to things, moving across the street and into the shadows of the cemetery as soon as possible. Sure every minute she would hear Tom and his friends coming back, she moved as fast as she could, but not so fast she would call attention to herself if someone else saw her. Finally, after what seemed an age, she was at the little gate. Fortunately no one was around. It wouldn't be easy to get all of her things in. She shoved one bag in quickly, then the other. Finally she pushed herself in behind and settled everything deep in the bushes. There at last she could let herself rest a few minutes, catch her breath, and let her heart settle down. It was a while before she was ready to move again, and then she took her things to the back door of the old house in several trips.

It seemed like forever before everything was inside. But finally it was accomplished. For the first time since she had heard Tom Williams speak, she relaxed, felt a little easy. She was safe. But what now?

≈ 4

BEST to get settled. With sure but quiet steps, Lucinda carried her things upstairs. Once there, she had the feeling that the house and even the land beyond, the cemetery proper, were welcoming her. It was almost as if she were being drawn in and made to feel comfortable and accepted. She laughed quietly to herself about feeling at home in a cemetery. Well, it was all right. She had nothing against it, as long as she wasn't a permanent resident.

Before she put her things away, she decided to check out the house. Cautiously, because she still did not know what schedule the man on the scooter followed, or if there were more guards besides the one man, she took her flashlight and looked around the first floor of the house. There was no evidence that anyone had been there since her last visit, more than a week before. Nothing had been moved. She stopped to examine Beloved Benjamin. What had his life been like? Nice, she thought, since someone cared about him so much. But why did he die? Kids then did die, more often than now, she thought. It seemed sad and unfair, though, when people had liked him so much.

Shielding her flashlight and holding the beam down, she examined the stones around. They were older than the Benjamin statue, and the people they had been made for had been older when they died.

Finally she moved back upstairs. It was beginning to rain again. She could hear it on the roof and against the windows. That was good. There would be less chance of someone's seeing her or her flashlight. She wondered if the rain would keep the kids out of her house, her real house, and decided not. The rain would help them, too.

With a sigh, she set about putting her things away. The extra clothes she put in the drawers in the dresser, also the towels and rags and things like that. The food she put on top, in its metal can, a protection from roaches and mice, if there should be any around. The dishes and kitchen things went into a separate drawer.

Everything was going very well. Of course, someone might see the can. But she couldn't worry about that. Anyone who came to the house now would surely know that someone had been there. There was no longer any way she could destroy all signs of her presence. She's just have to take her chances.

The one problem that remained was what she was going to do with herself. Her watch, the Timex Cherry had given her last Christmas, showed that it wasn't even nine o'clock. It was too early to go to bed. But what else could she do in the dark? Just sit and listen to the rain?

She glanced around, as if the walls of the room might give her an answer. And in a way they did. Or the door. She realized that if both of the bedroom doors were closed, she could sit in the hall and read by flashlight, and no one outside could possibly see the light. It would be just like home—books to read and no one to talk to.

She settled herself in the hall, her back against the wall and her feet out in front of her. It was quite comfortable, although it wouldn't be easy to write.

At first she thought maybe she wouldn't do any of her homework. If she had nothing to hand in tomorrow, it might please Rosella.

But on the other hand, that would be giving in. And she was so angry, in spite of being scared, that she didn't want to give in. Why should Rosella or anyone else decide for her what she would or would not do. It was bad enough that those kids had chased her out of her house. Why should they tell her how she should act, too? So she even did all the arithmetic problems. When she had finished, she dressed for bed and slipped downstairs with her flashlight, carrying it but not turning it on, and went into the bathroom.

There she did turn the flashlight on, keeping it away from the window so she could see to wash. The house was dirty, and so was she. It might be an idea to clean the place a little. Maybe in the morning.

Upstairs in bed, she lay awake for a while planning the next day. If she woke up early enough, she would clean some. But she'd try to leave the cemetery early enough to sneak home and see what had happened there. Then she'd go off to school by the streets that were most likely to have people on them, so she wouldn't be caught alone. When she got to school, she'd either go right in, or stay near the door where there was always a security man or a janitor watching. Doing something like that was not going to make her any more popular, but it might keep her safe.

In school she'd be all right, especially if she went to the girl's room only when everyone else did, and if she stayed with others. After school, if the kids followed her again, she'd go to the library and stay till it closed. She didn't think they would wait outside that long.

She was drifting off to sleep when a light passed the window—the guard on the scooter. It made the place seem friendly and secure. She closed her eyes and didn't even dream.

She woke once in the night, with the rain still pattering against the window and the roof, and a soft humming noise in the room, the same sound she had heard before. This time, listening closely, she thought it came from below. But there was no one there. Of that she was sure. She went to sleep again almost at once.

The next morning she woke up early enough to do some cleaning. She got the broom and swept the upstairs floor, dumping the results in an old vase on the first floor. Then she took an old rag she had brought, wet it, and went over the bed and the chest. The curtains she did not dare to touch, except to brush them off a little. The sun had made them fragile, and even a gentle touch might make them break apart. Of course, she couldn't even think of washing the windows. Someone would really notice that.

When she had done as much as time allowed, she washed, dressed for school, ate, and picked up her things to go. It was still raining and would be muddy outside. That meant she had to be careful not to leave tracks and also not to get herself too dirty. But she'd had enough practice getting under the gate that it went more smoothly than she had thought it might.

She moved cautiously around the corner, keeping close to the cemetery fence, and peered over at her house. It looked empty. No one was around, and it already had that deserted look abandoned houses have. She felt sorry for it. But it didn't pay to be careless.

She crept up to the house, onto the porch, and looked in the windows. As far as she could see, no one was there. The front door was open. The living room was a mess—cigarettes, beer cans, empty bottles, and the sweet, stale smell of pot. Ugh! She hoped she didn't have to come back again until her mother was home. Before she left, she packed a few more clothes and whatever else she could find that might be useful into an old book bag to take along with her to school. If she wasn't coming back, she might as well have as much from the house as possible.

Surprisingly, probably because it was raining, she had no trouble getting into school early. And the rest of the day went pretty well. She tried to keep in the background, and no one did seem to take much notice of her, although Rosella gave her a few strange looks.

One especially good thing did happen. In fact, it was such a marvelous thing she could hardly believe it. Ms. Pritchard gave her local history assignment. Lucinda put down Flowery Vale Cemetery as her project and after class asked for a note to give the gateman. Ms. Pritchard seemed impressed with Lucy's idea and gave her the note without question. She also said she'd get one from the principal if that should be needed.

The note not only promised help for Lu's security problem but gave her a better destination than the library for the afternoon. She could go to the cemetery gate with her letter. If she were lucky, the man there would talk to her, maybe even let her in. And once inside, no one could get at her. When she left, she would be so far from her usual haunts that she might be able to get to the store and then into her own part of the cemetery without being seen. She did need to go to the store. Her food was almost gone.

She had lunch with Kate and Pamela. Neither

seemed to have heard about her house problem because there were no questions from either. It seemed good to talk about ordinary things, like the stupidity of local history assignments.

It rained all day, and was still pouring when school let out. Lucinda didn't wait for anybody. She dashed away in quite a different direction from the one she usually took and wove around by all sorts of back streets until she was at the cemetery corner and down to the small door. Under cover of the rain, she slipped in with her books and the clothes she had taken from home in the morning, and was soon upstairs. From the back window, keeping as hidden as she could, she looked out. There was no one around. Good. She could do a few things then. And the first was to wash some clothes. She did it in the bathroom sink with soap she had brought from home, and hung everything on a string she ran down the upstairs hall.

By the time she had finished, it had stopped raining. But it was still cloudy. So it might be best to go to the gate right away. Taking her notebook and couple of textbooks so it would look as if she were coming right from school or the library, she slipped out and hurried along the fence, down one long side and around, to the main gate of the cemetery.

There seemed to be only one man at the entrance, seated inside a little guardhouse just behind the gates. A road went on either side of the guardhouse, one in and one out, she supposed; but one big double gate opened for both roads.

The man was reading a book as Lucinda stepped up

to his house with what she hoped was a shy, yet confident, look.

"I . . ." she began. The man looked up with a scowl. "In school," she began again. "In school we have this assignment. We have to report on local history, some place or something that happened in the history of this community. And I picked the cemetery. Because I live near. Over there." She pointed vaguely, in what she hoped was no direction at all. "I've wondered about it lots of times. And so I thought maybe you could tell me something. Or where I could find out. Here," she added desperately, as the man's expression did not change. "I've got a letter from my teacher, Ms. Pritchard."

She thrust the letter out, and the man took it. He glanced down quickly, then gave her a searching look, as if he were testing her out.

"Well, suppose I can help some. Not many people around on a day like this. Not many people at all, anymore. Not like the old days when people came all the time. No time to stop and talk at all then."

He rubbed his chin, and went on. "What you want to know?"

"Whatever you can tell me," Lucinda said. "When it was made. Who made it. Who's buried here—famous people, you know. What kinds of things are here—special things, statues and stuff. How you take care of it now." She added the last casually, hoping it didn't seem too far removed from a history research project.

"Well, we have this pamphlet with a map and a

little history. It doesn't tell everything, of course. You have to see the place, take time to walk around inside, to know what's here."

"Could I . . . Could I go in sometime? I'd be careful. Not hurt anything. There must be lots of interesting things that have to do with history, inside."

That seemed to cheer the man up. "You're right," he said. "Not many cemeteries like this one. 'Course, it isn't what it was ten, twenty years ago. Then we had twenty men all the time, working on the grass, the trees, the shrubs, planting flowers. Now we got five men, lucky to have that. We got only one gravedigger now; and he works lots of time cutting grass in the summer, shoveling roads and paths in the winter. The others, most of them, work in the greenhouses in the winter. Same as they used to. But only five." He gave another frown, then brightened.

"Did you know we have our own greenhouses, so we can start plants for the fancy plantings early? Not so fancy anymore, though. Not enough money."

Lucinda thought he sounded like her father. But she didn't want the man to stop. His information was too useful. "It must be hard for five men to keep everything going," she said sympathetically.

"Darned hard. Lucky we got good protection, that it got put in before money got so tight. At least we don't have to worry about people sneaking in from outside. Some places got real trouble these days. Kids turning over stones, digging up flowers. Drinking beer, smoking pot, leaving a mess. We got none of that."

"How come?" said Lucinda cautiously.

"Oh, those big iron fences. They got electricity in them. You must have heard that. Especially at the top. Little wires, all electricity. You get a shock if you just touch the fence anyplace. But you get a bad shock if you touch those wires at the top. Go all the way around the place. One man does nothing but see that the wires are in good shape. Fence does more than ten men—or even dogs. And see those lower wires— about four and a half feet up? When they're touched, sometimes even when just the fence is touched, they set off an alarm bell. A great system. Even shows on a chart where the fence got hit. And you can't even dig under the fence—it goes down three feet into the ground."

"Sounds really safe," Lucinda said.

"Oh, it is. Like I said, one man on the fence all day. And at night, a man on a motor scooter. He checks all the paths and runs the fence once, unless he hears something, of course."

"Wow!" said Lucinda.

"Oh, we're all set. No unwelcome visitors here. But you didn't come for that. History, you said. Well, that's all inside for the seeing. You just have to keep your eyes open."

"Can I go in?" Lucinda asked.

"Sure, might as well. You got that letter. And I can't see that you could do much harm. Pretty wet to go today, though. Maybe you better wait. Here, take one of these maps and come back tomorrow if the weather's better."

He pulled out a map and opened it. "Now look here. You go down there first. That'll interest you most because it's where the kids are. Nothing but kids in this little plot down here. You walk down until you see an iron statue of a boy, called Beloved Benjamin. Of course that isn't the original statue. Somebody ran into the first one. Can you imagine driving too fast, losing control, in a cemetery? Anyway, that statue sits on a point of land, and right behind it are other kids."

"What did he die of?" Lucinda asked, unable to restrain herself.

"Who?"

"Benjamin."

"Diphtheria, I think. Lots of kids died of that. His folks were so cut up, I heard, that they buried him here, then moved away to forget. Couldn't find any trace of any relatives when the statue got knocked over and got its arms knocked off. But everybody kind of liked Benjamin, so lots of people chipped in to get a new one. The old one's still up in the caretaker's house, I guess. You can see that here on the map. Empty now. Used it for storage for a while, before this new tool shed was built. Too bad. Pretty good house. But no one wants to live in a cemetery anymore."

"This is interesting," said Lucinda. "You really know a lot about this place."

"Ought to. I been here fifty years. Well, look here, you come back again tomorrow, and I'll let you in. You can see for yourself what's here."

"Okay, I'll be back, Mr. . . ."

"Simon. John Simon. Be looking for you tomorrow."

Lucinda nodded and walked out the gate. She'd be back. More than once maybe. Mr. Simon was going to be all right.

She hurried to the nearest store, bought a few things that would keep well and taste good without cooking, and went back, under cover of fog and a light rain, to her own private cemetery gate. The only unprotected place in the whole fence, she knew now. She looked in all directions, then slid under quickly and ran around to the back door of the house. It was nice to be home.

≈ ≈5

LUCINDA wiped off a stone in the kitchen and sat down on it. She had learned a lot today. But the most important thing she had learned was how little she had to fear in the cemetery. People outside couldn't get in, except for little kids who probably would never think of coming in her own little gate. And the number of men working was so small that no one was ever likely to know she was there. As long as she was careful. She could get careless just because there was so little danger. But she would guard against that.

She could hardly believe it. Such a good place. Looking around, she realized that she could do some fixing downstairs, too, if she wanted. No one would know. No point in doing too much in the kitchen, especially since there was no place to cook and not even a sink. But she could clean the bathroom. That would help her keep herself clean, which she had to do so no one at school would get suspicious. There was still time to do some work before dark. It probably wouldn't be a good idea to use a flashlight a lot at night.

She went over everything in the bathroom with a cloth and water. Tomorrow she'd buy some cleanser if she got to the store. She didn't want to use too much of her soap. Everything was so expensive. She had to be careful if her thirty dollars was going to last for a week, or maybe even ten days.

When she finished the bathroom, she went upstairs and into the front room. In a closet, under the eaves, she found a chair, a nice old chair, all carved, with a wooden seat. She carried it to the back room, then changed her mind. She would put it in the wide part of the hall and bring up the one piece of furniture that stood downstairs, a little table. That would give her a place to read and do homework—a study, so to speak.

It was while she was downstairs for the table that she heard the humming sound again. She didn't stop to look then, but when she had her study arranged, she walked down and into the kitchen, where the noise seemed loudest. She noticed at once that the statue of Beloved Benjamin seemed almost to glow. Surely it hadn't done that before! She looked at it in horror.

It was nearly dark now; the days were growing shorter, and besides it was such a dark day. But the statue stood out clearly in the room. Strange, when it was black iron. She walked up to it and touched it. Her fingers tingled. It wasn't a shock, exactly, but something happened. She remembered the pipe she had covered up. Could that have electricity in it? She thought not. Yet what else could be causing this?

Suddenly she wanted to run away. She didn't need any more secrets, any more mysteries. But where could she go? Fortunately, neither the humming nor the glowing seemed to get any stronger. The light wasn't really bright enough to be seen from the outside. At least, she hoped it wasn't.

After a bit, she began to relax a little. Nothing bad seemed to be happening. And if there was anything wrong with her new living place, it was that it was lonely. Maybe Beloved Benjamin, now that he hummed and glowed, would seem like company. She decided to eat her supper with him. That way she could keep an eye on what was going on.

She made a peanut butter and jelly sandwich, took one cupcake from a package, and an orange. That would make a pretty good meal. The only problem was something to drink. She had bought nothing, because everything she could think of either needed to be hot or to be kept cold. Water would have to do. She put everything on a flat stone, the one she had wiped off earlier. Then she got a rag and really washed off one nearby, to make a sort of permanent sitting place near Benjamin. She sat down and began to eat, with her feet propped up against Benjamin's base. As she ate, she talked, in a voice just above a whisper. It wouldn't do to talk any louder. That would be careless. But it was nice to pretend to have some-one to eat with. To tell about the day.

She poured it out in detail: her plans, and the way they had worked. Her visit with Mr. Simon. And even something of her fears about the gang who had taken over her house. Once in a while she stopped talking, and then she almost felt as if Benjamin were answer-ing her. But that, of course, was silly. She was really talking to herself. It was only because that was a strange thing to do that she was pretending Benjamin was real.

Her supper was long over when she finally decided that she had told Benjamin enough, and had asked enough unanswerable questions. Benjamin didn't know any more than she did about where her mother had gone and when she would come home again. It was hard even to speculate. And as to what her mother would think if she came home to find Lucinda gone and the place taken over by Dean's gang, there was no way of telling.

She did her homework in the new "study," which worked very well, much better than sitting on the floor. And then she went to bed. The humming con-tinued downstairs, but she paid no attention.

It was between classes the next day when Rosella came up to her.

"Where've you been?" she asked bluntly. "Don't tell me you've been at Kate's. I know better. So where have you been hiding?"

Lucinda almost grinned, but caught herself in time.

What should she say now? "I've been around," she muttered finally. "I have my own places." And with that she skittered away. Let them wonder.

After school, though, she knew she had to be careful. They'd be watching.

"Kate, can I walk home with you?" she asked. "I haven't seen you much lately."

"Sure," said Kate. "I've been wanting to talk to you. Where are you staying, Lucinda? I heard what's going on at your house. Rosella told me. You're not staying while those guys hang out there, are you?"

"No," said Lucinda. "You know Joel and I had good hiding places. I'm using them, that's all."

Lucinda looked up and saw Rosella and Janice watching. She pretended not to notice and went on with Kate until they came to a store near Kate's house. "Got to do some shopping," she said. "I think I'd better do it here."

"I think I'll go on," said Kate. "You know my mother likes me to come right home."

Yes, Lucinda thought. But maybe Kate was also afraid to be seen too much with her now. It was hard to know what kinds of things Rosella was saying.

"Okay, see you tomorrow," Lucinda said, turning into the store.

"You tell me if you need help," Kate said as she left. But Lucinda had the feeling they were only words. Kate didn't want trouble with Rosella and Janice and the rest. Her mother got mad if there was any kind of problem and Kate was involved. There was no point in counting on Kate for help.

Lucinda bought what she needed, things she could carry easily, then took a careful look out the door. Had Rosella and Janice really not followed? Or were they hiding? She couldn't just stand around, so she dashed off down one street and across another, avoiding places people might expect to see her. And she seemed to succeed. She was out of breath, but alone as far as she knew, when she reached her own little gate.

The trip into the house with the groceries and out with only her notebook was made so fast and so secretly, she felt really proud. She wished Joel could see her. In a few minutes, she was at Mr. Simon's gate.

"Oh, there you are," he said as she walked up. "Couldn't be sure you'd come today." He got up from his chair and pointed down the road. "You still have that map?"

Lucinda nodded and took it out of her notebook.

"Go in then and walk around. See those kids buried down by Beloved Benjamin and whatever else you want. Then come back. Maybe I can give you some more help."

It was colder today, even though the sun was out a little. Lucinda had on her old spring coat, not her raincoat, but even so she felt a little chilly. She wandered down to the places Mr. Simon had talked about. Benjamin was there on a point of land, just as he had said. The new statue was just like the old one, except that this one had arms. They reached out in front, as if he were beckoning her to come to him. And in a way, he was, she thought.

Behind Benjamin were the graves of some other children, from babies just a few days old to boys and girls in their early teens. Sometimes there were several in a family who seemed to have died at about the same time. An epidemic, she supposed. Well, that wasn't so much of a problem anymore; today there were others. She sighed and started back down one of the roads toward Mr. Simon's gate. In the distance she could see the top of the caretaker's house. But the trees and bushes hid most of it. Here and there other roads and walks branched off the main road she was on. She looked down them and longed to explore everywhere.

There were even some spots where no one was buried, where there were big statues instead. She could tell that there had been flowers around them in the summer. In one place, she passed a man cleaning up dead flowers and raking leaves. She waved to him, and he waved back and smiled. He must be one of the five caretakers still around. Or maybe he was the gravedigger. She shuddered. But no, the gravedigger cut the grass.

When she got back to Mr. Simon, he told her about the lakes on the other side of the cemetery. "They've been here since the very beginning," he explained. "They were made by damming up a stream. As long as we get plenty of rain, they keep themselves pretty clean, running over the dams. There are some mausoleums over that way, too. With stained glass, even, some of them. If you can come tomorrow, you really ought to go over. Most of the famous people here are in those mausoleums."

He really wanted her to come back, she thought. He must be lonely. But didn't he think it was strange that a kid would spend so much time on a school report about a cemetery? Maybe he just didn't know much about live kids.

"I'll probably come," she said. "And thank you for everything."

On the side street, she let herself into her gate and the house, still marveling over how easy this had all become. She had seen one man working on the grounds, that was all. There were four more somewhere else. If she explored some part of the cemetery every day, maybe she'd come to know where all the men were, even learn their habits, so she could be sure to avoid them.

The house felt good. Warmer than outside. That was because, as the pamphlet explained, when they put in the greenhouses, they had put in an underground heating system that heated all the buildings. The caretaker's house had still been in use then, so it too was included. She was glad to know she wouldn't freeze if she were still here when it got really cold.

Beloved Benjamin was humming merrily in the kitchen. Not quite so loud as yesterday, but enough to make the place seem lived in.

"Hi," she said. "Saw your successor today."

Benjamin did not acknowledge her greeting. He

just went on humming. She wondered again what made it. But since nothing seemed changed, she decided once more that it couldn't be anything dangerous. It might even have to do with the heating system, though she didn't think the pipe under Benjamin was part of that.

She went to work in the bathroom with the cleanser she had bought, and it didn't take long to get things as clean as she thought she ought to make them. It wouldn't do to go too far. She wished there was hot water, but that was asking too much. Besides, she wasn't used to it anyway.

The cleaning downstairs didn't take long, so she went upstairs and did a few things there, too, while it was still daylight. And then she had nothing to do. She'd have to bring some more books from the library. For now, she took her reading book from school down to the kitchen, and just for the fun of it, began reading aloud to Benjamin. She sat on her gravestone, with her feet propped up against his base, as before. The tingle in Benjamin tickled her feet a little and made them feel good.

When it got too dark to read, she made a sandwich and took out some cookies and an apple and settled in the same place to eat, once more telling Benjamin about her day. The room was dark when she finished, except for the glow from Benjamin. It was not so much that he gave off light, she decided, as that he seemed to have a light inside him. It must be that old pipe, but she didn't understand why.

She was so intent on trying to figure out just what

made the light that she didn't notice at first that the sound from Benjamin was changing. It went from a hum to a kind of Morse code: blips and bleeps. And then the sound became almost words, queer unaccented words that didn't quite make sense.

Lucinda sat up startled when she realized what was happening. She reached out and touched the statue with her fingers, but the tingling had not increased.

It had started to rain again outside, after the good day. She couldn't remember when they had had so much rain. You'd think there could be more than one day of sunshine.

She tried to think about the rain. To remember when they'd had so much. But it didn't work. It didn't shut out those new sounds. What did they mean? Could the rain have something to do with them? She didn't see how. Unless they came from water dripping onto something. She listened hard and decided that that might be what it was. But where was the dripping? She couldn't see any water anywhere.

She didn't dare let herself be frightened. But inside she felt her panic rising. Once again she wanted to get away. But as before, there was no place to go. She left the kitchen and went upstairs, hearing as she went the sound change from blips back to a hum. Did she do it then, by being close? Or was someone listening, spying on her? That thought made her really afraid. She buried herself in arithmetic problems, but she couldn't concentrate. What would happen if she had to leave here?

Benjamin was still humming when she went down

to the bathroom later. She tried to ignore him, but couldn't. What was she going to do? For one thing, she took some water with her, in case she was thirsty in the night. No point in coming down oftener than she had to. Back upstairs in bed, her sleep was troubled. Benjamin and Tom Williams were both after her!

It was the middle of the night when a noise brought her fully awake. At first she didn't know for sure what the sound had been. Then she realized it was a kind of "pop" from below. She listened, stiff and strained, waiting for more sound. But none came. Her sleep after that was even more fitful. She dreamed of lights and hums and specks of color that were not color. When her hand touched the wall once, there was a tingle that woke her up; but she did not stay awake, though she wanted to. It was as if she were being willed to sleep, to a restless sleep, by something outside of her. Were there really ghosts after all? she wondered. Were they upset because she was stealing into their cemetery?

In the morning she woke up as usual at dawn. It was still raining and misty. Generally she felt wide awake and ready to go when it got light, probably because she went to bed so early. But this morning she felt heavy and uncertain. She got up and dressed slowly, then pulled the bed together with a precision she had ignored once she learned how little the house was used. She ate upstairs, not down, and washed with the water she had brought. It took a while to gather up her books and papers and make them ready to go out in the rain. But finally there was nothing left to do. Reluctantly she went down, the stairs, taking each step slowly, seeing how quietly she could move. Checking every corner of the house she could see on the way down, to make sure no one was there. Nothing had changed.

She tried not to glance at Benjamin as she went by. She felt as if he had betrayed her. There had to be some good reason for the noises. But she didn't know what it could be. Or maybe she was imagining too much. She ought to go to Kate's that afternoon, just to keep from being alone. But she knew she wouldn't. She was afraid of questions and of giving away her secret.

It was all too much. She was confused and she knew it. It was because she had slept so badly. The noise was getting to her. That was what it really was. Benjamin and his hums and pops were disturbing her sleep.

She went to the bathroom, then slipped out and started toward school.

≈ **6**

"LUCINDA, I don't understand you, what have you been doing lately? Where do you go?" Kate stamped her foot.

Lucinda hadn't meant to meet Kate. By going early, she had been avoiding everyone. But all that slowness this morning had put them at the same corner at the same time. And now they were in the middle of a fight. Kate wanted her to come over after school, and Lucinda said she couldn't.

"I've got things I have to do," Lucinda said. "It's . . . I can't explain it. You know about Tom Williams' gang and all."

Kate exploded. "You've been going with them, haven't you? That's what you've been doing, Lucinda Gratz. You're hanging out with them. I never thought you would. I never did. And my mother, too, she said you were too smart for that. That's why she let me have you over all the time. She said you were okay, and you needed us. But that's not so. You're just like Dean. Just like him. And you'll wind up where he is, too. You're dumb, Lucinda Gratz. Just dumb, dumb, dumb. And my mother won't let me see you anymore."

"No, listen. You don't know what I've been doing. I can't tell you. But it's okay. Kate, listen!"

"I will not listen. If it's okay, then why can't you tell? You don't care if you're my friend or not. And I don't care either." Kate started to run.

Lucinda ran after her. "Listen, Kate. I do want to be your friend. But you have to trust me. You know I wouldn't do what you think . . . go along with that gang. I couldn't do it, Kate. I couldn't."

It was no use. Kate was running faster and faster. And she wasn't even trying to listen. What had happened since yesterday afternoon? Had she had another talk with Rosella, or had Kate's mother heard something? It was impossible to know.

Left alone in the light drizzle, Lucinda felt as if she ought to turn around and start the day over. Everything had been going so well, and now it was all falling apart. Benjamin—all her friends—were doing strange things. And she was tired and afraid. Was it time to tell someone? No! Not if it meant some city agency and a horrible foster home. That would be worse than anything Benjamin, or anyone, could do.

School went slowly, too slowly. She felt menaced on all sides, except by the teachers. And that was even more awful. It wasn't that she didn't like them. They were mostly okay. But having them so approving all the time made her feel set apart, not one of the kids. Just when she wanted to be like everybody else, to disappear into the crowd.

It was still raining when school was over. Which matched her mood. Bad luck everywhere. As she dashed out the door and moved away from school in one of the evasive patterns she had developed, she wondered if anyone else had ever become so good at slipping in and out of places unseen. Maybe she had a special talent for it. But what did you do with a talent like that? Become a criminal? It was not a cheerful thought.

The library was where she was going, she decided. She had to have some kind of live company. And Ms. Clipp was always glad to see her. Though that might not last long either, she thought gloomily. Not the way things were going.

"I have a book for you," Ms. Clipp said. "It has a lot in it about the history of this area, and I think you'll find some material there about Flowery Vale."

Lucinda couldn't say that she didn't need it anymore, that she had found a better source of information than anything the library could provide. So she took that book, then looked through the children's room for some other books to take, too. She wanted books that would take her mind far away.

When she left the library, she had the local history book, a book on American national parks, and another one on travel in Peru. She had also taken a novel about a girl who lived in 1870. That might help her understand more about the people who were buried in the cemetery.

From the library she went straight to the cemetery, keeping her eyes open for trouble and finding none. Maybe the kids had given up looking for her. More likely it was the rain. They were probably warm and dry in her house. Though she hardly thought of it as her house anymore.

It seemed almost too late to visit Mr. Simon, but then she decided she would. She left her books in the kitchen, carefully ignoring Benjamin. She didn't want to know what he was doing, though she couldn't help but notice that he was humming.

Mr. Simon was in his little house, reading as usual, when she came up.

"Hello! Gave up looking for you today. Nasty weather, isn't it?"

She nodded and said, "I almost didn't come. But I didn't have anything else to do." Then in a burst of confidence she went on to tell him as much of the truth as she dared. "My mother works. She's not home in the afternoon. And I had a fight with my best friend. And there's a bunch of kids, a kind of gang, that hangs around my house, and I'm scared of them when my mother's not there. It feels better to come here."

Mr. Simon nodded slowly. "You want to see the lakes today?"

"Can I go in the rain?"

"It isn't raining now."

Lucinda looked out. It was still overcast. The ground was soggy and wet. But the rain had stopped.

"You go over this way." He took out another copy of the map, since she had brought only a pencil and paper with her. "You'll pass the war memorial. Then there's a nice little bridge over the stream, and you can see down the whole of the Lake of Repose and to the dam. Some of those mausoleums are right beyond. You might want to go over and look, copy down some of the names." He glanced at his watch. "There's time if you hurry. I don't always leave right at five."

Lucinda moved slowly down the road, looking at both sides, but not stopping. The war memorial wasn't much. Like a lot of other statues. But she stood finally on a bridge over the stream and looked down the lake for a long time. It seemed marvelously misty and wonderful, with a shifting green and orange haze at the shores, from the fall trees. The mausoleums beyond were like quaint, but elegant, little houses. She walked over the bridge and looked at them more closely. One of them even had a little porch.

What had they been like, she wondered, the people inside? Ladies who danced at grand balls? Men and women who lived in great houses full of furniture and ate huge meals served by hordes of servants? Well, maybe not. But surely their lives had been fine. She wondered if she would have liked being them, living then. It might have been nice.

She took a different way back to the gate. On either side of the path there were statues of angels and vases with scarves draped over them. Not close together. Nothing here was crowded. Everything was spread out and elegant.

Partway to the gatehouse there was a big statue called *Peace*. She had passed it yesterday, but now she stopped to look. The other big statues had been of stone, but this one was metal of some kind. She touched it and felt the same tingle she had felt when she touched Benjamin. What a relief! Obviously whatever was happening in Benjamin was everywhere in the cemetery. She didn't have to worry about him then. He was simply a part of something going on all over. This statue didn't hum or pop, but perhaps Benjamin just did that because he was inside.

She stood for a moment at the peace statue and looked around at the trees, the shrubs, the paths, and the monuments, then hurried on to the gate.

"Oh, it's lovely, just lovely," she said as she opened the door to the gatehouse.

"It is, isn't it," Mr. Simon said. "Well, you come here as often as you want. Makes it seem a little like the old days, when people were around all the time. You just think of John Simon as a friend when you need one."

"Oh, I will," said Lucinda. "Thank you."

"You come back now."

"Yes, I will," Lucinda promised again. Then she ran down the block and around the corner. She wondered what Mr. Simon would think if he knew the whole truth. In a way she felt bad about what she'd been doing. He'd been nice to her. But maybe he wouldn't really mind about her living in the house. It was the sneaking in that he wouldn't like. She'd better be careful about how much more she told him. It wouldn't pay to get too friendly, not until her mother came back, anyway.

Feeling better now about Beloved Benjamin, she entered the house quite boldly and even said a rather brash hello. Then, although the sounds he was making were odder than the ones of the day before, she sat down with the new library books and began to read aloud to him again. It seemed silly when she thought about it. But the sound of a voice, even low and quiet and her own, was better than no voice. She was half-way through the book on the national parks when it got too dark to see. It was going to rain hard again. She still wasn't confident enough to put on the flashlight regularly anywhere but in the upstairs hall. So she closed the book.

At that moment, from deep within Benjamin somewhere, the odd noises stopped, and then a mutter came through the silence that sounded almost like "Don't stop."

Lucinda jumped to her feet in terror! There *couldn't* be anyone here! Or could there? What was under the house? She didn't think there was a basement. But there might be a small one of some sort. Yet how would anyone get down into it? There were no steps outside. She glanced around the room, looking to see if there was a trapdoor in the floor. But if there was, she couldn't find it.

"What is it?" she murmured aloud, trying to pull herself together. She mustn't panic.

"What is it?" The sound again came from Benjamin, very hesitant and unsure. Almost like the voice of a little child.

"Benjamin?" she said uncertainly. There were no such things as ghosts. Of that she was sure. Otherwise, she would never have stayed in the cemetery at all.

"Benjamin," the voice said. More confident now.

Lucinda held herself rigid. Why did it repeat what she said? The first time it hadn't. Though maybe she hadn't understood.

Then the voice came again. "What are those trees?" it said very slowly.

Lucinda did not reply. What could you say to an iron statue that talked? She stood frozen, unable to move. What should she do? Then slowly, almost without willing it, she reached out and touched Benjamin. She had gotten so used to the light and the tingle, she had almost forgotten about them. As she felt the ripple in her fingers again, she wondered, could Benjamin somehow be connected up to something that made him like a radio? Was she hearing someone with one of those CBs?

Benjamin had a pleasant warmth to him now, that he hadn't had before. The tingle was there and the light, the glow, but there was more. Something from inside him seemed to reach out and touch her as she touched him. Something almost reassuring. Her fear seemed to drain away, but she didn't know why. And that in itself was frightening. She pulled her hand back.

"Who—what are you?" she asked hesitantly.

"Don't know," said a voice. She wasn't sure if it was in her ears or just in her head.

"Then where are you?" she asked more confidently.

"Don't know," said the voice.

"Are you real?" she asked desperately.

"Real?" The voice sounded puzzled, if a flat, mechanical voice could have any expression.

"Are you alive? Do you exist?" she asked.

"Yes, real. Yes, alive."

"Are you trapped under this house?" she said. "Or are you somewhere else?"

"Not trapped. Reaching out. Here and somewhere else. Come through, but where to? Can you know what I say?"

"I don't know." She was now more puzzled than afraid. Was it like a radio? "You speak English. Are you in the United States?"

"English?" Clearly the voice was curious. "United States?"

"Well, you must know about English, since you speak it." Was someone playing a joke? But how could anyone get into the house? And it couldn't be anyone who belonged to the cemetery. All the men who worked here were old, she thought, too old to play a joke like this. It *must* be one of those CB things.

"On what planet are you? In what system?"

"Don't joke with me. How could I be anywhere but on Earth?" She almost laughed, but couldn't quite manage it.

"Planet. System. What word?"

"What do you mean?"

"What group? You understand?"

"I'm in the sixth grade," she whispered. "Is that what you want to know?"

"No, in your language, best I can do after listening, putting words in program, maybe mean star system?"

Were there really ghosts then? Did spirits from another planet or some other place come here? Did people come back to where their bodies were and not know anymore where they were? She shuddered. Maybe the stories you heard about graveyards were true!

"We are the closest large system, we believe. Have we come to our neighbor, as we wished? We have been close. Very close."

"Neighbor? Star system? Are you a radio operator?"

"Wish to know more of your words. English, you say. The talking and the reading, good. We put sounds in, use what maybe you call machines. Understand. But do what you did before. Touch or whatever. When there was a being together."

She reached out and touched Benjamin again, wondering if she was doing the right thing. Would she be shocked, or even electrocuted? But there was still only the gentle tingle and the new warmth. And again that strange feeling inside.

"Better. Easier." The sound was louder now, more complete, as if it came from closer, which was strange since it had always come from Benjamin.

"Now let me make you understand. But what sort of being are you? What part of your thinking group are you?"

That was the strangest question yet. What part of her thinking group? "I'm a child," she said finally. "A girl. I go to school to learn. I am not grown up."

The voice seemed to accept this as a proper answer. But it also held a kind of sigh, the sort of sigh an overworked machine might make. "We break through to a child," it said. "But we must use what we have. Now tell me this: Where in the great patterns of star groups does your group lie?"

Lucinda thought hard. She hated, for some reason, to disappoint the voice, to let Benjamin down, even if it wasn't the real Benjamin. But what did he want to know? The star group? Did he mean the solar system? Or something bigger? "Do you mean our sun and the planets around?"

"What is the sun?"

"The sun is our star. It gives light and solar energy and all that stuff. We see it in the daytime."

"Yes, but of what group is your star a part?"

She drew her fingers from the statue a moment to think. Maybe he meant the galaxy, the Milky Way. Joel had told her some things about that once, how almost all the stars you see in the sky are a part of the Milky Way, and that is our galaxy.

"I think," she said, "the sun is a part of a galaxy. Lots and lots of stars. It's called the Milky Way."

"Yes, that's it: the galaxy. But which one are you? Where are you? What other galaxies are nearby? Spiral, elliptical, round?"

"I don't know. My brother would maybe. But he's not here. I could try to find out for you."

"That sounds good," said the voice. "Will you be here again?"

"Oh, yes, I'm here all the time now."

"Good. We hope to be here for a time, too. This is the best we have done. Something where you are is right for us. So we must learn what we can from you. Or can you bring someone else to where you are, someone who knows more about your galaxy?"

Lucinda was horrified. That she could not do, no matter who Benjamin was.

"No," she said, very sure of herself, very positive. "Only I can come here."

The voice seemed to sigh again. Then it went on. "Can you get more of the kind of information you have been giving us, the things you have been reading? Can you bring the words that will tell us about your planet, your sun, and your galaxy?"

"I can go to the library and see what books I can

≈ **85**

find," she said. "I'm not sure what they'll have, but there has to be something."

"That is good, and now will you go on with the book you were reading? We are receiving your words well. Our machines are using them and making it easier and easier for us to talk to you. Anything you read will help us."

Even that she was not sure she should do. But she decided she could be careful with her flashlight, shining it just on the pages of her book, and she could read a little while longer. She went upstairs, got the flashlight and some things for supper, and came back down. As she ate, she read the rest of the national park book. Then she explained why she could not go on reading too long, her situation in the house, as best she could. And the voice seemed to accept and understand what she said.

"But tell me who and what you are," she asked.

The voice hesitated. "It is hard to explain to you, when I use your language so badly. I do not have all the words I need. But we think we are of another galaxy, one near you, but we cannot be sure just how near. We have made a new discovery, one that lets us send messages in a new way, using energies that are not bounded by the speed of light, and that can leap across the space between galaxies very quickly. But we do not yet know how to control our discovery or to determine in what direction our messages are beamed. Therefore, we could be in our own galaxy still. But we doubt it. We think you may be in the nearest large galaxy, the one with two small galaxies beside it, but we are not sure."

"You aren't from a planet then?"

"Yes, we too rest on a planet most of the time. But that is of lesser importance to us."

"You don't have to stay on one planet?"

"No, we can move from one to another if we choose. We have machines to take us."

"You must be really far away."

"Yes, we believe we are far, for us. But for the whole of what exists, we are close, we think."

That was too much for Lucinda. She felt tired. "I think I need to go to sleep now, or at least do some work in my language arts workbook," she said. "Do you mind? I'll try to bring some books tomorrow that will help you."

Once upstairs, she made sure the doors were closed, and then she turned on the flashlight in the hall. She wished she had a mirror so she could look at her face. Maybe then she would know if she were crazy or not. Could her mind be playing tricks on her? Maybe because she was alone so much? But even if she were crazy, how could she have thought up something like Benjamin? Who could think of a statue talking like that?

There was no answer, and to keep from trying to find one, she buried herself in her language arts workbook. Now and then, from downstairs, there came odd burps and gurgles. These, too, she tried to ignore. And because she wasn't afraid anymore, she succeeded pretty well. There was no point in getting excited about something she couldn't do anything about. And until tomorrow there was nothing she could do about or for Benjamin's voice.

She even managed to get to sleep, maybe because the whole business of Benjamin had made her feel so tired. But once again her sleep was troubled. As if something from far away was mixing into her thoughts and giving her strange dreams.

When she got up in the morning, she was not sure she really wanted another day to start right then. The only good part was that it was Friday. Maybe if she could get through it, and have the weekend to think, she'd come up with some answers. And it wasn't, she realized, only Benjamin that posed questions. He was only her newest problem. What she really needed was someone to talk to, someone who was real and not just talking through a statue.

≈ **7**

LUCINDA didn't see Kate that morning, but if she had, it wouldn't have made any difference. Kate wouldn't have spoken. Why hadn't she told Kate the whole story? she asked herself. Would it have mattered? Yes, it would. Kate would certainly have told her mother, and then there might be a foster home. In her imagination, she could just see how dreadful that would be. Now she could at least hope she would see Cherry or Joel again. Besides, she had promised to give her mother a week or ten days. And she meant to keep that promise.

She was almost glad the weather was still awful: misty and dull. It isolated her as she walked, and seemed to separate her from out of the world. And that's where she felt she belonged. The things that were happening to her just did not fit into any kind of everyday pattern.

She spoke to no one when she got to school. Increasingly that seemed the best plan. She was early, but as usual she did not stop at the playground. Instead, she went straight to her locker, put in the library books she had brought to return after school, took out the things she needed for the morning, and went to see Mrs. Fernetti, who taught her class arithmetic and science. Mrs. Fernetti was just hanging up her coat when Lucinda arrived.

"Yes, Lucinda," she said, looking not too pleased to see someone so early.

"Mrs. Fernetti, I need to know about the earth and the sun and the Milky Way. I have a kind of project, and I just need to know. It's important. Do you know a book I can read? One that I can understand?"

The look on Mrs. Fernetti's face changed from mild annoyance to amazement. "I remember Joel," she said. "He was a good student. And you do pretty well, Lucinda. Very well lately. But somehow I didn't quite expect this from you. If you want to do some extra work in that area, I can give you some books and tell you about others that you may be able to get at the library.

"Look here, Lucinda." She moved to the blackboard. "This is what our solar system is like. And this is where it is in our galaxy, the Milky Way." She quickly drew some circles, but before she could explain very much, the bell rang. "I'll have the books and list for you when I see your class today," she promised as Lucinda turned to leave.

Lucinda groaned as she walked down the hall. As if it wasn't bad enough that she was keeping up, now she was going to do extra work. Unless she could keep it very quiet, there was more trouble ahead. But she couldn't let Benjamin down, not when he was counting on her. She'd just have to be careful. What would Joel have done? she wondered. He would have been more help to Benjamin certainly. But she wasn't sure he could have handled the rest any better than she had.

Mrs. Fernetti's gift of two books and a list of other books did bring a sneering comment from Rosella and a look that said "Just wait." Well, she would wait, Lucinda thought. And maybe after the wait, it would be Rosella who was surprised.

"How are you coming with your cemetery project?" Ms. Pritchard asked in the hall, at the end of the day. Lucinda hoped she was the only one who heard, but she couldn't be sure. Rosella and Janice were nearby.

"Fine," she said, deciding to ignore the others, and glad to talk about one of the subjects that was on her mind, even if she couldn't say much. "I've been talking to a man at the gate, and he knows a lot. He lets me walk around inside and tells me what to look for. I've got a lot of good notes. It's a nice place, Ms. Pritchard, really nice. Peaceful and quiet. I can't explain it, but I like it there."

Ms. Pritchard smiled absently. "Well, have a good

time. I know you'll write a fine paper. Your work has been excellent these past weeks, Lucinda. Several of the teachers have remarked on it."

Lucinda smiled and glanced toward the outside door. Rosella and Janice were gone. To some place far away, she hoped. She said good-bye, and as she walked to the door, she thought about what Ms. Pritchard had said. Have a good time doing research on a cemetery! Didn't teachers ever stop to think about what they were saying? And yet, in a way, she *was* having a good time in the cemetery, wasn't she?

When she got to the outside door, she saw Rosella and Janice and a couple of others waiting for her down the block, but it was so easy to give them the slip she almost laughed. The special route she chose that day began at some well-placed bushes on the school grounds and took her a block out of her way but got her to the library with no trouble at all.

Ms. Clipp was surprised to see her back so soon.

"I had some books that I was through with," Lucinda explained. "And I need some more books for a special report in science."

"Another special class assignment?" Ms. Clipp said in a tight voice.

"No, just me. Some extra work," Lucinda said.

Ms. Clipp smiled.

"Mrs. Fernetti gave me these books. But she thought maybe these would help, too." She handed Ms. Clipp the list.

"We don't have all of these. But we do have one or

two of them, and I may have some newer ones, some that Mrs. Fernetti may not know about."

Lucinda left the library with three more books. With the two Mrs. Fernetti had given her and her regular schoolbooks, she was loaded down. She needed to stop at the store, but she didn't see how she could carry any more, especially since it had started to rain again and she was trying to protect the books with her umbrella. Maybe at the store they would have a plastic shopping bag. That might make it easier.

At one corner she looked down the cross street and saw Rosella and a boy named Jon. Lucinda hid until they were out of sight. Then she moved as quickly as she could through yards and vacant lots and all sorts of places until she got to the store closest to the cemetery. There she bought what she needed and asked for a large plastic shopping bag. It cost fifteen cents, but it was worth it. It held everything, and she got to the house with no difficulty at all.

She dropped off the groceries and most of the books, but kept a few to take with her to Mr. Simon. It would look better, more realistic.

She had her umbrella up as she hurried down the sidewalk to the corner and then around to the main gate. It was misty now, more than raining, but she didn't want to get any wetter than she had to. Near the gate she thought she heard someone behind her. Not daring to look, she began to walk faster and then almost ran.

"Whoa," Mr. Simon said as she came up to his door breathless.

"Had to go to the library again," she said. "Another special assignment. But I wanted to come here even if it was late." As she spoke, she glanced out and saw Jon walk by. Had he seen her? Was Rosella near? Or even Tom? Jon didn't stop. That was good.

"Glad to see you, Lucinda. Gotten used to your coming."

"Will you be here tomorrow?" she asked, still trying to see if anyone else was going by. She had to calm herself and listen to Mr. Simon's answer. The main reason she had come was to find out if she could visit the cemetery on the weekend.

"Nope. I work five days a week, just like everybody else. Almost nobody here on Saturday anymore. Used to be as many here then as on other days. But now, Saturday and Sunday there's only two. Sanders runs around checking the fence, goes on the night man's scooter. And Johnson is at the gate. You want to come tomorrow? I'll tell Johnson about you then. And I'll let Sanders know, too."

That was a lot more than Lucinda had asked. And it told her all she needed to know.

"I'll come tomorrow if I can, or maybe Sunday."

"Good then. I'll tell Johnson. And look here at the map. You go to the Crown Chapel if the weather's better. Nice up there. Maybe Johnson will give you a key so you can get in. If he can't find it, though, go anyway. Good view from there. It's right on top of the big hill. Highest place around."

Lucinda nodded. She'd see what would happen. No one else had come by. She ought to hurry back to the house while she had a chance. Jon might come back.

"Got to go now," she said. "Got things I have to do before my mother gets home." It wasn't exactly a lie.

"Well, go help your mother. And watch out for those young punks. Take care now, you hear?" said Mr. Simon. "See you on Monday. And I'll tell Johnson about you."

She nodded again and went off.

It was early to leave. Not much past four in spite of all she had done. But if they were looking for her, it was best to get in to safety. And besides, she wanted a good bit of daylight for reading to Benjamin, if the voice was still there. She crept down the street and around the corner, her umbrella closed in spite of the continuing mist. So far so good. There was no one on the street that she could see. If she hurried then, she ought to be okay.

When she came to the small gate, however, on a quick impulse she went beyond. Keeping close to the fence, she almost crept along, all the way to the corner, and peered around at her own house. It seemed deserted. She moved on toward the house, still keeping close to the fence, ready to run or to hide if necessary. But there seemed to be no one around. Across the street from the house, she became convinced that it was empty, at least for the present. Maybe they were all out looking for her. Or maybe they really only came at night.

On a further impulse, she ducked across the street

and up on her porch. There was no sign of anyone. She tiptoed over and opened the door to peek in. The inside was a mess: beer cans, the heavy smell of pot, and all kinds of trash everywhere.

She stepped in. Was there anything she needed while she was here? If there was anything left! She moved cautiously through the rooms. They had been everywhere, those punks. She laughed to herself. She was beginning to think like Mr. Simon. But in the living room, something on the floor caught her eye: a crumpled piece of paper. It looked as if the writing on it was Joel's. She picked it up, smoothed it out, and sure enough it was a note from him. He had written her a letter. She had never thought of that. Had there been other mail? she wondered. What else could have come? A letter from her mother? She thought not. Bills maybe? She couldn't worry about that.

Wanting to read Joel's letter, and not daring to stay and read it there, she hurried out the door, across the street, and back to the shelter of the fence. Just in time. She had barely reached the corner when she saw Tom and Jon come up beside the burned-out house. She skittered down the side street, grateful again for the rain and the mist. She shouldn't have taken such a chance. But it was nice to have Joel's letter.

At the small gate, she glanced quickly in all directions, then hurried through and to the back door. It was good to be home.

≈ 8

THINGS were not the same in the house. She saw that
right away. Had someone been in? Her breath clung
to her ribs. Could someone still be there? Then she
realized that it was more a change she could feel than
one she could see. Nothing had moved. But Benjamin
glowed red. The sight alarmed her. After dark, the
man on the scooter might see. She'd have to tell those
people, or whatever they were, not to come through
so strong.

The hum that came from Benjamin was more even,
more orderly than it had been before. She tiptoed
over, still not sure that everything was all right.
Reaching out, she touched Benjamin and was flooded
with the warmth she remembered. Yet even that was
stronger than it had been.

"Good, you have returned," said the voice. "And do you have information for us?"

"I hope so. I have some books that should help."

Without even going upstairs, she settled on her tombstone and began reading. The best book, she decided, began with the earth and the solar system, and then went on to talk about the Milky Way and even the galaxies beyond. It was short and not too complicated. It took about an hour and a half to read it all and describe the pictures and charts to Benjamin. The voice said little while she read and talked.

"That's a help," said Benjamin when she stopped at last. "Too simple, perhaps, but quite a clear picture, if our grasp of your words is correct." Then he asked some questions about what she could see at night, stars and such, that Lucinda found hard to answer.

"You can't see anything here at all?" she asked.

"No, I can only get your words, but sometimes I see things as you picture them in your mind. When you do something. I'm not sure what. But it's the thing that tells us you are there without your speaking."

"It must be when I touch the statue, when I touch Benjamin," she said. "I'll try to do it all the time. But you mustn't make him glow so bright, if you can help it. Someone might come and see. And I explained how I'm not supposed to be here."

"We'll try to keep it down," said the voice. "Now tell us, Lucinda, how much mathematics do you know?"

"Only as much as a sixth grader," she said, getting into a position in which she could keep part of her hand on Benjamin.

"Which means that it probably won't help us much," said the voice. "Is that what you are saying?"

Lucinda giggled. Benjamin had been only seven when he died. And now sixth-grade arithmetic was far too simple for him. "Benjamin, you're too much," she said.

The voice picked up on that at once. "Benjamin. Ah, yes, the statue of the child. I suppose it does seem strange to you to have a statue of a young child asking such complicated questions. But do call us Benjamin. It will be easier for you than thinking of us as just a voice."

It did seem more like talking to a person when she gave it a name, instead of just thinking of it as Benjamin's voice.

"Have you another book to read?"

It was almost dark because the day was so bad, but Lucinda decided she would take a chance with the flashlight again, at least for a while.

The next book she chose was one about the galaxies, the Milky Way and others, and about the whole universe. It was harder to understand than the first because everything it talked about was so big. But Benjamin didn't seem to have any trouble with it.

"That's good," he said after she had finished the first few chapters. "That helps place you. You are our neighbor, I'm sure of it."

When Lucinda decided she had better not take a chance with the flashlight any longer, she found herself just talking, telling Benjamin all of her problems, repeating what she had said before and going on to explain in greater detail.

"We got some of that before," Benjamin said. "I wish we knew more about your culture so we could be of help. It puzzles us. We do not understand."

"I wish I could help you more," Lucinda said.

"It's not your fault. You are giving us all you can, and we are grateful for that. The very fact that we have come into your galaxy is exciting for us—just to know that intelligent creatures exist where you are and to learn something about you is more than we had hoped to do so soon. Our equipment is not yet perfected. Something where you are is right for us, has helped to make our visit possible."

"Maybe it's the rain," said Lucinda. Then thinking quickly, she said, "Yes, it must be. I first heard the humming after all this rain began. And there's the electricity." She explained about the fence.

"You may be right. That may have something to do with it. It may have set up just the sort of electrical field we need for you to receive us—not too strong, not too weak. Well then, we must do as much as we can while it rains."

"Tomorrow is Saturday. There's no school. I can stay part of the day, or maybe all day. It's not like—you know—anyone is looking for me."

"Mr. Johnson will be looking for you."

That was true. And she might need to do a little more shopping. Her flashlight batteries weren't going to last forever. With that she realized that she hadn't eaten supper yet, and she was hungry.

"I—I've got to go upstairs now," she said.

"All right. We'll be waiting for your signal, your touch, anytime you are ready to return. And while we wait, we have what you've read to us to review."

Upstairs, she made a sandwich at her desk; and while she ate, she went through the other books she had—library books, schoolbooks, everything—picking out the things that would be best to read to Benjamin. There was no point in repeating things. She made notes and put strips of paper in certain pages. Not just science things, but things about people, too. Then she got to thinking about solar systems and galactic neighborhoods and knew what she wanted to write for Mrs. Fernetti.

It was so clear in her mind that she wrote it all down and then went on to plan her cemetery paper for Ms. Pritchard. The ideas fell together so nicely it was fun—like doing a jigsaw puzzle. She couldn't write all of the paper for Ms. Pritchard because there was still more information she needed to find. But it was good to have it planned and partly written.

It wasn't until she was finished with that and was beginning to be really sleepy that she remembered the letter from Joel. How could she have forgotten? Her very first letter from him.

She pulled it out of her coat pocket and smoothed it

on the desk as well as she could. The letter was not long.

Dear Lucinda,

How are you? I'm fine. This is a nice place. I'm in a room with two other guys. It is pretty noisy, but okay most of the time. The food is good, but all the guys complain about it anyway. I don't complain because I don't think I should. But maybe some day I'll say something, just to be one of the guys.

I think about you pretty often. I wonder how things are going for you. Have you had to go to the new place? I hope not. If you did, was it okay? I don't think you would be scared, but it might be sort of strange.

Well, I have to do my math now. The subjects are all hard here, but not too hard. Write and tell me what is happening at home.

Love,
Joel

It didn't tell much, but it did make him seem closer. If the gang had read it, and she supposed they had, she wondered what they thought. Had they wondered about the "new place"? She wished she could tell Joel about all that had happened. She wondered what he would think of Benjamin. She ought to write and tell him everything. The letter wouldn't get there right away. Her mother should be home by the time he got it. She tore out a sheet of notebook paper and told him briefly what had occurred in the past week. But in the end, she decided not to tell him about Benjamin. He might get all sorts of strange ideas about what was happening to her if she did.

By the time the letter was done, she was really tired. As she undressed for bed, she wondered if she should have told Joel about Benjamin after all. But it would be hard to explain it in writing and make it sound real. Her last thought as she went to sleep was that she didn't have an envelope for the letter; she'd have to buy one tomorrow.

The next morning she got up very early. It was not raining, but it was still cloudy. It was too early to go anywhere, so she dressed, ate, washed some clothes, and read to Benjamin the rest of the book she had started the night before.

At about eight o'clock she stopped reading and got ready to go out. The rain had started again, so she put on her raincoat and got out her umbrella.

Carrying what money she had left, she went off to a drugstore and a supermarket that always opened early. Between the two, she was able to get the food and other things she needed. The drugstore had a stamp machine, so she got some stamps, addressed an envelope she had bought, and put a stamp on it. It was ready for the first mailbox she saw.

Then in one corner of the drugstore she saw some paperback books: a few children's books and some adult novels. That was something she hadn't thought of. If she read Benjamin some fiction, he might understand better about the people on Earth. She bought a children's book and an adult book, one she had heard someone mention, about things that happened in the government in Washington.

She mailed her letter to Joel and got almost to her gate when she saw Tom Williams and another older boy down at the corner. They saw her, too, because Tom pointed, and they both hurried toward her.

What should she do? There was no place to go, and she was weighted down with her bag of stuff. She couldn't just drop it and run. Almost all her money was gone. She needed what she had bought.

Furtively, trying not to give away her secret, she moved on toward the gate. But what would she do when she got there? Her mind raced over the possibilities. Then, at the last minute, as she came to the gate and had to decide what to do, she heard a voice down the street calling Tom. Both boys glanced away, and in that brief moment she was through the gate and into the bushes. She couldn't see out, but that didn't matter. They couldn't see in, either.

"Lucinda," Tom shouted then. "Come here, you fool kid. Don't think you can get away. We know you're around. We know you've got some 'new place' to hide around here."

She shivered and kept as still as she could. Would the business about being scared in Joel's letter make him realize that she was in the cemetery? She heard both boys running. And then there were others, too, talking loud, trying to make her think they were almost finding her, so she would come out. But the more they searched, the more she knew that they did not know where she was.

Finally they seemed to drift away, although she

couldn't tell if they had left someone behind or not. She peered out carefully and saw no one. So, with infinite caution, trying not to move a leaf, she crept to the back of the house under cover of the bushes, and then made a dash for the back door.

Once inside the house, safe and with her groceries intact, she collapsed, breathless, to the floor. That was a close one. And the danger was not over. They might not know where she was. But they knew she was near. Why did they think they could get back at Dean by doing something to her, if that was really what they wanted? Didn't they know he couldn't care less what happened to her? But she supposed they had to feel they were doing something. Well, they could find someone else to take it out on. She was not going to get caught.

When she looked at her watch, it was just a little after nine. She had been gone only a little over an hour. But it seemed like years. As soon as she felt able, she put her food away in the metal can, put on dry clothes, and went back downstairs. She might as well plan to read to Benjamin all day. For a whole lot of reasons, she did not intend to leave the house again. If it rained and was foggy, Mr. Johnson would not expect her.

She sat down on her customary stone, put her feet up against Benjamin, and the glow in the statue grew deeper and the voice came.

"Hello. That's what you say, isn't it? We've been waiting for you. Tell us one thing. How much of your time has gone by since you talked to us last night? That will help us compare your time with ours."

"I think it was about eight-thirty when I went upstairs last night," Lucinda said, trying to remember. "And now it's about nine-thirty in the morning. So that's thirteen hours. There are twenty-four hours in a day. And seven days in a week. Fifty-two weeks in a year. A year is the time it takes the earth to go around the sun."

"Very good," said Benjamin. "That's what we needed to know. And now, do you have more to read to us?"

"Yes, I can read all day. It's raining, so no one will expect me anywhere."

She went through the special nonfiction books first, reading the things she had marked the night before. Some of what she read she understood, some she didn't, but it all seemed to please Benjamin. She was not finished with those until early afternoon, with time out for lunch and an occasional drink or a question from her listener.

In the middle of the afternoon, she began the adult novel about the government. It was longer than she thought, but Benjamin seemed interested, so she went on and on. Some parts were dull and didn't seem to be anything that would be of value to someone in another galaxy, so she skipped them or read them quickly herself and summarized the action. She read all the parts that had to do with people actually doing things for the government though, and sometimes Benjamin asked questions she couldn't answer. She realized she didn't even know exactly how laws were made, and then what happened afterward. The book made it all sound very complicated.

Once in a while she got up and walked around the room to stretch her legs and rest her eyes and her voice. Then she'd think of questions she'd like to ask Benjamin, but she didn't dare take the time. There was so much she had to read him, so many things she wanted to make him understand.

"This is fine," Benjamin said once. "It really is a good thing you are a child, Lucinda. We need to learn as a child learns."

That sounded polite. But she didn't really believe it. Benjamin was just trying to make her feel good. She worked harder than ever after that though, and as she went on with the Washington book, she began to wonder what other things she ought to be sure to read: The schoolbooks she had marked, both for the information and so that Benjamin could see what schools here were like. The children's fiction book. And then there were the hard parts of the science books that she had skipped. What she really needed was an encyclopedia. She could just see herself bring in the whole set from the library through that little gate, with Tom or Rosella watching. She shuddered, but she laughed, too. One thing, they couldn't follow her. They were both too big.

When night came, she was exhausted. But before she left Benjamin, she decided maybe now she could have a turn at the questions. She got herself a sandwich and an apple and said, "Now, can't you tell me something about where you are? Do you have bodies like ours? Trees? Oceans? Cities? What's it like over there?"

"That is hard for us to tell you, Lucinda. Because we know other thinking creatures, other civilizations in our galaxy, we can stretch our minds to understand a little of what you are like. But you have had no such experiences, so you will have difficulty imagining thinking creatures who are very unlike yourself. Yet we can try to help you see us a little. Of course, we have what you would call plants, growing things that make their own food. They are unlike yours, but the basic idea is the same.

"Our home planet has less gravity than yours, we believe. For that reason and others, our plants and our own bodies are different from yours. Quite different.

"You would feel strange here, Lucinda. Yet I think you would have to agree with us that we too have beauty in our surroundings and in our lives. Slow winds blow over our world, slow but with great power, and because of the way we are made, we can drift with them from place to place. We have no need of transportation on our world. We are born, grow old, and pass on to—we know not what, just as you do. Our government is planet-wide. It must be because we move so easily. But it is not always perfect. We do not all agree here, any more than your government people do. Perhaps a perfect government cannot exist anywhere."

"You have children?"

"Yes, surely."

"Do they go to school?"

"Not in the same way you do. Your school seems to be group teaching in set patterns. You go, and you learn specific things that it seems wise for you to learn. Everyone learns more or less the same things. Am I right?"

"Yes. That sounds right."

"Our children, on the other hand, are individually led into experiences that teach them many different things in many different ways. Each learns according to his needs and by direct experiences. They find their learning in many different settings. But then movement from place to place over long distances is easier for us than it is for you."

"You said you've seen other places in your galaxy. Are people there more like you or more like us?"

"Like neither. Each thinking group has its own shape and culture. Yet, for all intelligent life there seems to be something underneath that is the same: a restlessness, a desire to grow, a reaching for something more than we have."

Lucinda was quiet for a moment. She would have to think about that. "Are your children ever left alone?"

"In some learning situations. But not as you seem to be—in a casual way. This we do not understand."

Lucinda sighed. She didn't understand either.

"What kinds of odd people have you seen?" she asked, changing the subject again.

"No group is odd to itself. But we have seen many that seem odd to us. One group we know well can change shape at will. They shape the matter of which they are made into whatever form suits them or their occupation of the moment. They can change as often as they like."

"That sounds neat. I'd like that. There are lots of times when it would be great to be different: bigger or smaller, taller or shorter, pretty . . ."

"Seen or unseen, at rest or rolling in the wind, like one's companions or very different. Yes, it would be useful. Pleasant, too."

The discussion went on to things that Lucinda found more difficult to understand. In fact she did not understand a great deal of what was said. But she tried to remember, and even made some notes, because she wanted to think about some things. And maybe someday to ask some questions of somebody on Earth. The more she heard about Benjamin's world, the more she thought she would enjoy it.

"Are there other galaxies, too?" she asked at last.

"Of course. You read about them yourself."

That was true. But it was hard to think about. Millions of suns in the Milky Way. And millions of Milky Ways. It made her feel small. And yet it made her feel big, too, because in her mind she could hold such a big idea.

"But why did you come here, out of all those places?"

"Because you are close—in a relative way. But remember, we did not really choose. We sent out, and something where you are—the field made by the fence and the rain perhaps—brought us there. We have reached your planet now. If we break through again, we may be at a place that does not even know of your solar system—or maybe even your galaxy. I think we have talked of this before."

"Yes," said Lucinda. "But it all seems so special, and so chancy. I don't know how to understand it."

"Just think of us as Benjamin, coming to you from a long way away. And someday, perhaps, you will come to understand more."

"Then you really are Benjamin. You are in him. That's why he glows."

"Perhaps."

"Whew! I guess that's about all I'd better ask. I'm too tired to think about anything more. There are more books to read. But I don't think I can spend all day tomorrow, unless the weather is really terrible. If I think I can get out without those kids seeing me, I should go to see Mr. Johnson. Mr. Simon will think it's funny if I don't go either day, since I asked special. But I want to talk to you some more, too. Maybe when I've been asleep, I'll be able to think of more you ought to know, and more I want to know. Do you need to sleep?"

"We rest, yes. And we understand your needs. You have been very good to us today, Lucinda. Rest well."

Lucinda was so tired, even though she hadn't done anything but sit and talk and read all day, that she went right to bed. She went to sleep and dreamed of distant galaxies, creatures that changed shape, and worlds with lovely lifting winds. It was a pleasant night.

≈ ≈ ≈ ≈ ≈ ≈ ≈ ≈ ≈ ≈ ≈ ≈ ≈ ≈ ≈ ≈ ≈ ≈ ≈ ≈9

MORNING brought sun into Lucinda's eyes. The sky was not entirely clear, but the dawn sun broke through and came into the window in a very welcome way. Lucinda stretched and yawned, turned over, and went back to sleep.

She got up an hour or so later, dressed, washed, and ate. She was getting tired of her sandwich, cookie, apple and orange diet. Even an occasional carrot did not help. She had bought a quart of milk and drunk all of it the day before, because she had been thirsty doing all that reading. And because she had no place to keep it cold. Today she would have to drink water. And as for food, she would have to make do with what she had. The nearest store open on Sunday was too far away, and in too dangerous a direction to chance going. Besides, she didn't have much money left.

It was too early to go anywhere. And she didn't think she was ready for Benjamin yet. So she sat down and finished her homework, and did a little more on the cemetery paper. Once, all of that would have seemed an odd thing to do, but now it seemed marvelously normal. Something that kept her firmly tied to Earth. She needed that. She had to keep her mind here, to remember who and where she was, no matter how strange her life had become.

When she finished, she decided she was ready to spend an hour or two reading to Benjamin. Then she would go out, before too many people were around, and see Mr. Johnson. She would talk with him and have a picnic in the cemetery, maybe up by the church Mr. Simon had talked about. When she'd seen all she wanted to see, certainly by the middle of the afternoon, she'd leave and try to get back without being seen.

If things looked very clear, and she knew after yesterday that she had to be careful now, she might try to get over near her real house, to see if by any chance her mother was back. It was, after all, nearly a week since she had gone away.

The morning went as she had planned, though she spent more time with Benjamin than she thought she would. She read the textbooks and part of the children's novel, and then talked a little about things she knew.

It was nearly noon when she left the house. She

knew she didn't have to be too careful inside the cemetery. There was only one man inside. But there could be more people in the houses across the street on Sunday. And, of course, the gang could be looking for her, now that they suspected she was near. She crept out carefully. Her movements had gotten so quick, so furtive, that she really thought someone would have to be looking very closely to see her. Yet she had no reason to be overconfident. Tom Williams had seen her yesterday.

She saw no one on the street until she got almost to the main gate. Then, to her horror, she saw Rosella and Jon in the distance. She knew that they had seen her, too, and she began to run. Before they could come anywhere near, she was right at the big gate. But it was closed and locked!

For a moment she thought there was no one there, that she was trapped; but then she saw a man in the guardhouse. She called out, "Mr. Johnson. It's me, Lucinda Gratz. Mr. Simon told you about me. Remember? Please let me in."

He ambled out of the door of the guardhouse and came to the sidewalk gate—not the large one for cars, but the small one at the side for pedestrians.

Lucinda glanced quickly in the direction of Rosella and Jon. They had stopped at the corner and were watching her with smiles on their faces. They thought they had caught her, because, of course, children never got into Flowery Vale Cemetery.

Then Mr. Johnson opened the small gate, and she walked in. He closed the gate behind her at once.

Lucinda wished she could have both walked in and looked down the block to see the expressions on Rosella's and Jon's faces. But she had to be content with just going in.

"Got the gates locked today. A little problem here."

Had they discovered the electricity, the thing that was in Benjamin?

"Kind of a flood," Mr. Johnson went on. "Over to the lakes. Sanders worked on it yesterday; working there today, too. All that rain. Looks as if the dams might go. Wouldn't do much damage. Lakes aren't deep. But better to be careful. You'll do all right, though. Simon says you do what you're told. Writing a paper, he says. Looking for information about the place."

"Yes," she said, relieved that he was going to let her stay. "For school. I'm sorry about the flood. Is it bad?"

"Not really flooded yet. The lakes are high. Dams are old. Sanders is sandbagging them. Stay away from that side of the place, just in case; and don't go too near the stream down at the south end."

Lucinda nodded. "There's one thing I'd like to know. Where are the oldest graves? I want to copy what it says on some of the stones, to put in my paper."

"Well, the oldest are right in here, below the gate, on either side of Elm Road, between Promise Walk on one side and Sunset Walk and Memory Way on the other. Just beyond the Hope monument."

Lucinda thanked him and moved on. He wasn't as talkative as Mr. Simon, but that was all right. She was just glad he had let her in. One thing for sure, she was going to be able to do what she pleased inside today. No one would pay attention.

But Rosella and Jon! Would they wait for her to come out? Surely not till afternoon! But if they did, what would she do? She couldn't just go to the care-taker's house from inside. She had to leave, or Mr. Johnson would wonder. Moving down into the area Mr. Johnson had pointed out, she tried to put her worries out of her mind and concentrate on grave-stones. She did find some that seemed very early—1851 and 1852—and copied what they said. But Rosella and Jon stayed in the back of her mind.

In a short time she decided that gravestones from a long time ago were not very interesting—at least not these. They didn't say much but "Rest in peace" or "God's sunshine in our lives" and things like that. She felt restless and upset. She had to know what was hap-pening outside, what dangers she might face in leav-ing the cemetery. What should she do? What was it Mr. Simon had said? That the church, Crown Chapel, was on a hill, the highest place around? Maybe that's where she should go. She might be able to see out.

She pulled the map from her coat pocket and plot-ted the quickest way to Crown Chapel. Luckily, it was in the safe part of the cemetery, where there was no danger of flooding. She moved on quickly.

The day had stayed nice. The sun was out full now,

and the clouds were almost gone. It wasn't warm exactly, but she felt comfortable enough in her coat. It was nice to be outside.

She paused here and there to read old markers, even though she was anxious to get to the top of the hill. Some of them were from Civil War days. She wondered what life had been like then. Had it been as hard as now? There was a war, of course. That made problems. She copied down some of the inscriptions as she passed.

Finally she found herself at the base of a steep hill, which, she decided, had to have the chapel on top. The road wound up, and on the way there was a pretty statue of an angel on one grave, blowing a trumpet. A little farther on, another group of graves had a stone bench right in the middle. She wondered who was supposed to sit there.

The road eventually led into a path, a walking path that was just wide enough for one car. She supposed sometimes people had to be driven up to the chapel. But most people were supposed to walk.

Tall trees rose on either side now, and in summer, she could tell, the walk was lined with a narrow band of flowers. Beyond the flower beds, the grass grew taller than it did in other places in the cemetery, almost wild, but not quite. The whole scene was like something in a book, alive and full of wonder and beauty. It seemed miles from Tom Williams and Rosella and the rest. It was hard to believe they were so close.

The curves of the path became sharper and the ascent steeper. Finally Crown Chapel lay just ahead. It was a small building, made of brownstone, with a red tile roof. There were stained glass windows on all sides, and a door in the center of the front. She walked all the way around the squat little building, admiring it.

She had forgotten to ask for the key, but she tried the front door, and to her surprise it was open. Inside there were five pews on each side of the narrow center aisle. Chandeliers hung from the pointed ceiling at the front and the back. At the front there was a raised platform with a pulpit at each side, and a carved table in the middle.

She sat down on a pew to rest a minute and to take it all in. It was a long time since she had been in a church. They had gone with her grandmother, and after her death Cherry had taken them once in a while. But she and Joel had never gone alone.

For a long time Lucinda just sat, not even thinking of her problems, just letting the peace of the place fill her. She was glad she had come to the chapel. It made her feel good inside, as if, if she tried hard, everything would come out right. The problem was what to try. And finally she decided that the thing she had to do was to go out and look for Rosella and Jon and whoever else might be around.

There was a wooden bench outside, so she sat down to have her lunch. She opened her sandwiches, then looked around. You could see beyond the cemetery all right. Not all around, because there were trees in the way. But the view was pretty good. Her own house was right down in front of her. There was no one there that she could see.

She glanced toward the main gate, turning around to look. The street there was partly hidden by trees, but she could see enough to know that Rosella and Jon were nowhere near the entrance itself. Then she looked the other way, examining her house more carefully. Rosella had come from somewhere and was now sitting on the porch, as if she were waiting for someone. Maybe she thought that Lucinda would have to come home sooner or later. If she thought that, Lucinda decided, she was in for a surprise.

Looking around again, she discovered Jon, sitting on the curb near the main gate. She had missed him in her first look around. Why was he waiting? Why did they care so much? What would it do for them to catch her? Was it like a game to them? Maybe. But that didn't change the fact that they were after her, more in earnest now, it seemed, than before. It was possible that the mere fact that she had eluded them so well had made them more determined.

Looking keenly now, she saw other kids scattered around outside the cemetery, some of them playing ball in the street, others just sitting. They couldn't all be waiting for her! That was silly. But why else were they there? This wasn't where those kids generally hung out.

She decided that whether or not they were all there

waiting for her, she had to assume they were. It wouldn't be a good idea to think anything else. Which meant that somehow she had to get back to the cemetery house without their seeing her. And that seemed almost impossible.

What would happen if she got caught? She couldn't even imagine, but she felt sure it would not be something pleasant. And she realized all too well that if she disappeared, no one would know. No one knew where she was, or that she was alone. She wished now that she had called Cherry. She had written to Joel, but he wouldn't know if she disappeared. So what help would that be?

Forcing herself to think calmly, she began to plan. As long as she was in the cemetery, she was safe. It was outside that the danger lay. Yet she couldn't just stay in the cemetery, because Mr. Johnson would expect her to leave. When she left, even if she could outrun whoever saw her, even if she got to her little gate before anyone caught her, her hiding place would be discovered. And probably lost.

She sat thinking hard, no longer even chewing on her apple. There had to be a way out. But only one solution came to mind. She had to somehow leave Mr. Johnson's gate, then come back in the same gate without his knowing. Go to the house from inside. But how could she manage that?

She gathered her papers together, both her sandwich papers and notepapers, and put them into her carrying bag. She could work out what she was going to do better if she were near the gate, she decided.

Hardly realizing where she was going, her mind intent on her problem, she started down the hill and missed the turn at the place where the path joined the road. For a moment she panicked when she found herself in a great clump of bushes. The path was overgrown, and she couldn't see where it led. But on the other side of the bushes was Elm Road. She came out across from a group of mausoleums, like the ones near the Lake of Repose. And at one, a car was stopped.

So Mr. Johnson was letting in some people, maybe ones who had come a long way. She stood hidden behind a bush, looking at the car. If only she had a car that would take her far away. But wishing wouldn't get her anywhere. Only her feet would. And her head. It was good to know that there were people in the cemetery. That might be a help. She thought carefully. Would the car stop at the gate so the people could talk to Mr. Johnson? And when he opened the gate for the car, could she quickly go out, and then come in again while he was watching the car? It meant taking a chance. But maybe it would work.

She stepped out onto Elm Road. Walking past the mausoleums, she saw that the door to one was open and someone was inside, two people in fact, sitting on the little bench there. She hurried on. She must get to the gate before the people decided to leave, in case they were the only ones all afternoon.

She almost ran. The tombstones no longer interested her at all. And the statue of Peace seemed unimportant. *Hope,* up near the gate, seemed more appropriate.

She paused behind the statue, in a place where Mr. Johnson could not see her if he was looking in her direction. She needed to plan. The car would leave by the right side of the gate. If only it would stop. Actually it would have to stop, since the gate was closed. If the people talked to Mr. Jonnson then, she could hurry past, say a quick "Bye, Mr. Johnson" as if she had somewhere to go, dash out, and sneak back in, slipping by on the other side of the gatehouse.

Her thoughts centered on this one project, not trying to think of anything else. But the car did not come. How could people sit so long in such a little place? And when they came, would they wonder why she was standing there? She was in plain view of Elm Road. She moved along the side of the statue to a place where she would not be so visible. Then she just stood.

It seemed as if years went by before she heard the sound of an engine. But it didn't seem to be coming up Elm Road. It was on Circumference Drive, coming from the Lake of Repose. But no one was allowed to go that way because of the flood. Peering out, she saw a truck. It must be Mr. Sanders. He pulled up to the gatehouse and stopped. Mr. Johnson came out and slowly opened the gate. Then he walked toward the truck. How long would he stay there? She darted around and saw that Mr. Sanders and Mr. Johnson were having a conversation. Mr. Sanders—at least she assumed it was he—was leaning out of the window of the truck cab. This was her chance! She walked quickly down the road past the truck, on the other side of Mr. Johnson.

"Bye, Mr. Johnson," she said.

Both men looked up.

"Bye, Lucinda," said Mr. Johnson. Then he turned back to Mr. Sanders. "You think you can get more sandbags on a Sunday? You really need 'em, with the rain stopped?"

"The lakes are still rising, and there's a lot of water running into that creek above here. If we don't hold some of it back, that culvert below will overflow, and then we'll really have a mess."

The words hit Lucinda's ears, but she didn't sort them out. It didn't matter what they said, as long as they kept on talking, kept looking at each other. Mr. Johnson had pushed the right-hand gate open, but the left-hand gate was nearly closed. She walked out of the open gate, past the little concrete island that separated the way in from the way out. There was a crack of space just big enough for her in the left-hand gate. With one quick movement, she stooped down low, so the gatehouse would hide her from the men. Then she all but crawled back into the cemetery. If the men were looking, they might see her, she knew. But she hoped they wouldn't.

Now the truck was pulling away. In a panic she dashed across the entry road and into a clump of bushes that stood near the fence. It was not a heavy clump, but it might hide her. She drew herself in and made herself as small as possible, so she would not be seen either from inside or outside.

For what seemed ages, she held herself rigid, still. Lucky her coat was dark, and her hair. Mr. Johnson was in his house again, and the gates were closed. But he was so close. She was sure he would see her if he looked hard. And what about Jon? Had he heard her say good-bye? Heard Mr. Johnson say good-bye? Was he looking for her? Would he think to look inside the fence? She shivered, and then realized that not only was she scared, she was cold. It was getting colder, even though it was only midafternoon. She'd always thought of October as warm, but it wasn't today.

Another sound! A car. Where was it? Was it coming in? Would the people see?

No, it was the car from the mausoleum, and it had to stop. Mr. Johnson stepped out, opened the gates, and then turned to speak.

Lucinda slipped slowly and carefully through the bushes. She knew from the map that she was between Forget-Me-Not Trail and the outside fence. And as far as she could remember, there were bushes all along the fence. If she could move a distance from the gate through the bushes, then maybe find an easier way to move on toward the house, she might make it.

How many people might be in the cemetery? Mr. Johnson was the only one she knew of for sure. But that didn't mean there weren't some other visitors. Once she got to the old house, though, no one would bother her.

It was a long half hour from the gate to the house,

ducking and hiding all the way, pausing to listen. Afraid she would be found, either from inside or from outside. She saw no one, but heard voices from the street. She stopped dead still in the nearest sheltered place every time she heard one. It was a good thing the cemetery had so many big bushes, she thought. There were lots of places to hide. But the bushes weren't warm. She was getting colder and colder. Though maybe it was just that she was so afraid.

Finally the house was in sight, and then at last she was inside. She fell to the floor, feeling as if she had been gone a hundred years. It amazed her that the place looked the same. What had she expected? Yet how could she feel so different, and this not be different, too?

She moved to her sitting stone and to Benjamin, who glowed as before. She touched him, and he spoke. Thank goodness something was normal!

Without stopping to think, she poured out the whole story of what she had seen and done; the words tumbled out in a maze, though she didn't know what she expected Benjamin to do. If he even understood.

"This is hard for us to understand. Your ways are not ours. Can they do harm to you, these people?"

"Oh, yes. Yes, of course. They could hurt me. I don't know how—what they would do. But I don't want to find out."

"You can spend the rest of the day and the night here, since no one knows where you are?"

"Yes, I will do that. But I don't know what to do tomorrow. If they should be around in the morning, I won't be able to go to school. They're at my house most of the time now, I think. And they know I'm near. They'll keep watch. And . . . and . . . I don't know what they'll do. What I should do?"

"I . . . we . . . would like to help you, Lucinda. But our picture of your society is not yet clear enough. We cannot advise. Except that perhaps you should read some more to us. Get your thoughts away from the situation. Maybe then your mind will show you new things, things your fear now hides from you."

They were right, she realized. She was not thinking clearly now. She was too excited, too tense. It was a miracle she had gotten to the house safely. If one miracle had happened, maybe another would, too. Or maybe, if she was quiet, she would see some way out.

≈ ≈ ≈ ≈ ≈ ≈ ≈ ≈ ≈ ≈ ≈ ≈ ≈ ≈ ≈ ≈ ≈ ≈ ≈ 10

IT WAS late afternoon. The kitchen of the old house was growing dark because the sun was far to the west. It was the living room that held the last light of the day. But Lucinda stayed in the kitchen, reading to Benjamin in the quickening twilight. She had long since read all of the things she had that were of real value, but they were both enjoying the children's novel and the selections she had chosen from her reading textbook.

She glanced up, realizing how late it was getting.

"You were right. This was the thing to do. I feel much better. But I think before it gets completely dark, I ought to go out and take a look around. I want to see my house, my regular house, in case my mother has come home. If she has, she'll wonder where I am."

"Be careful. Don't be seen if you can help it."

She was out the door quickly and quietly. It was quite a bit after five. Mr. Johnson and Mr. Sanders should both be gone. But there was the night man. She had never really learned his schedule. Maybe he'd be busy with the flood. Taking no chances though, she slipped into the bushes and moved through them, down and around the corner to a place across from her house. She had never been there before. She was close, and yet seeing the house in a very unaccustomed way. It didn't look the same. It was sagging and run-down. Alone and neglected. She felt almost as if she were looking at it as a stranger, seeing it for the first time.

There was one light on inside, but she couldn't tell who was there. Even if her mother was home, there was no way to know it, unless she came to the window.

Then suddenly Lucinda heard voices from the sidewalk on her side of the street. She drew deeper into the bushes.

"She could be at Kate's," someone said.

"No, they had a fight. She wouldn't be there. Besides, I saw Kate and her family go off someplace. There's nobody there today. Lu has to be around here."

"Could she have gone to Cherry's?"

"No way! Listen, Cherry doesn't want Lucinda around where she is. She's got a good thing. Why queer it with a kid sister?"

"She's got to be around here, I tell you. How come

you lost her, Jon? You said she left the cemetery."

"I was down the block. But I heard her say good-bye. Heard the old guy at the gate say her name. I wanted to let her get a little way from the gate, so she couldn't run back. But then she wasn't there at all. She couldn't have seen me. I don't know where she went."

There was a whole bunch of them. They walked across the street in the middle of the block and sauntered up onto her porch. A couple of them went inside, but the rest sat on the porch and on the steps. They began talking about something else, and finally they were laughing and yelling at each other.

"You kids get out of there! I've had more than enough of you this week!" It was crabby Mr. Winski. Lucinda had always hated to see him coming. But now she felt more friendly.

"Aw shut up," one of the big boys shouted.

Mr. Winski muttered something and went back to his own house. But the kids grew quiet. Maybe they were afraid Mr. Winski would call the cops. Lucinda couldn't hear what they were saying now, so after a bit she decided there was no sense in waiting. It was clear that her mother was not there.

The kids were getting noisy again as she left. And once more she heard Mr. Winski.

"You kids get out of there, you hear? You get off this block before I call the cops." He hadn't really left his own yard this time, and he carried something. She couldn't tell if it was a stick or a gun.

There was a low grumble, and the kids got up and started moving down the block. But Lucinda knew they would be back. In fact, they would probably just walk down the street a little way and then sneak back and inside. Once they were in the house, Mr. Winski would leave them alone. He was obviously a bit afraid of them.

Should she go out and tell Mr. Winski what was going on? She hated to. But her mother might be in danger if she came home and walked into the house and those kids were there. Maybe Mr. Winski could do something. But then Lucinda remembered more about him—the cross old man and his cross, nosy wife. Neither one of them would believe her. She had better stay where she was.

She turned and made her way back to the cemetery house. She was tired and hungry. There were bread and cheese, some cookies, maybe some carrots, a few apples and oranges. That wasn't what she wanted though. Something cooked, hot. Well, there'd be school lunch tomorrow, if she made it to school.

She ate with Benjamin, describing what she had seen. The more she talked, the more discouraged she got. She had been so sure she could win out, could keep herself safe until her mother came back. Now she wasn't so positive. But she was more determined than ever that those kids were not going to lay their hands on her. If she had to starve to death in the cemetery, she'd do that before she'd let herself get caught. Still, there had to be a better way out than that.

"Can't you take me where you are?" she said finally to Benjamin. "I don't want to stay here any longer. Things are different where you are. Why can't I go there?"

The voice in Benjamin almost laughed. "That's when your problems would really begin," he said. "We have our problems, too. They're just different from yours."

"It never sounded as if you had problems. And anything would be better than this."

"Change can be helpful sometimes. But not as much change as your coming here. Besides, we have no way to bring you."

"You came here."

"Not in ourselves. Just with a mechanical voice. We are not in Benjamin, Lucinda. It just sounds to you as if our voice comes through him. You know that. We've talked about it before. But even if it were possible for you to come to us, there would be no way you could live here. You probably couldn't eat our food. We do not look at all like you. You couldn't drift on our winds. And you couldn't even speak to us, because our way of communicating is different from yours."

"You're just making excuses." Lucinda knew she was being unreasonable. But she was tired. And it was so hard to decide what to do.

"No, not excuses. Telling you the truth. We wish we could help you. But it simply is not possible. And soon we will not be with you at all. Indications are that our association with you is growing less distinct. The fine day, perhaps. Or other things we have not yet discovered. Nevertheless, something is changing."

Even Benjamin was going. Lucinda thought she had never known such despair. There would be no one left. She began to cry. What would she do?

"Rest, Lucinda. Sleep. When you are rested, the answer may come."

There was no point in staying in the kitchen. Benjamin was no help. She went upstairs, began to go through the motions of undressing. It was too early to go to bed, but she didn't want to do anything else.

She had become used to undressing in the dark. Everything was placed so she knew just where things were. She wondered idly if that was the way blind people managed. She felt blind, even though she could see in the usual way. What she needed to see and couldn't was the future. Was it true that there were troubles everywhere? She glanced out the window, where the moon shone through the trees. All those people out there in the cemetery. Did they have as many problems when they were alive? She didn't think so.

She turned to the bed, crying again, weary with thinking. At least in bed it would be warm. This house might be heated, but it felt cold tonight.

She fell asleep finally, too tired to worry any longer. But the dreams that came seemed worse than the worry. She kept waking up afraid, but she could never quite remember what it was that she was afraid of.

What was that noise? She jerked awake again. It wasn't a dream this time. There was a noise. Someone in the house? No, thank goodness, outside. But what was it? Fire sirens! Had she left something downstairs that might burn? No, of course not. Had someone seen the glow from Benjamin? No, the engine wasn't stopping here. But it sounded close. And there was more than one. She went to the window, not really expecting to see anything, but there was a red glow over the trees. In the direction of her real house!

Her house! Could those crazy kids . . . ? No, they wouldn't burn a house down. They had more sense than that. But they could have left a lighted cigarette somewhere or . . . There were lots of things that could have happened. If it was her house. That was what she had to find out.

She threw on her coat over her pajamas and slipped on her shoes. Down the stairs and out the door, hardly thinking what she was doing. But even in her haste, once she was outside, she kept to the bushes. The man on the scooter might want to see the fire, too. She moved by the same route she had used at sunset, picking her way between the bushes and monuments. And at last she stood, well sheltered, watching her house burn down.

The tears slipped down her face. It was the only home she had known. It was where her grandmother had lived. Where all of them had been.

The fire must have had a good start to be burning so fiercely. Had the gang all gone? She had thought

134 $\approx$

that some of them might stay all night sometimes. But if someone had been there, she didn't think it could have gotten to be such a big fire. Unless they meant . . . But no, she didn't think they would have set it deliberately. She could believe a lot of things about them, but not that.

She couldn't really see the house very well because there were so many fire engines and firemen in the street. And other people were coming, too.

"Anybody in the house?" a man's voice shouted.

"Not that we saw," a fireman shouted back, one who seemed to be in charge.

"Listen," yelled another voice, Mr. Winski. "There ought to've been a kid and maybe her mother. Ain't seen 'em around much lately, and there's been a gang of kids hanging around all the time. But there is a mother and kid supposed to be there."

She heard a flurry of activity. Windows breaking at the back of the house.

"There goes the roof!" someone shouted.

A great shower of sparks, like Fourth of July fireworks, shot into the air. Clouds of smoke poured out. Lucinda gave a gasp, but stifled a cough. And it was a good thing she did, because just then she was aware of the light of the scooter. She pulled herself in close to the center of a bush, glad once again that her coat and her hair were dark. She hid her face, pulling herself into a dark ball. But the light didn't touch her. The man got off the scooter and moved to the fence about a hundred feet from her. She held herself still, knowing she couldn't move until the man had gone.

It seemed like hours. She heard the voices, heard the people wondering where she and her mother were. The firemen were sure no one had been in the house. Then some people began wondering if her father was gone for good. Talking about them all. It seemed strange, to be standing there in the cemetery and listening.

Above it all was the sound of the firemen, the noises of trucks pumping water, of axes chopping away at her burning house, of men shouting warnings to each other. How could she be so still when her house was burning? Yet, what else could she do?

At last the flames died down; one fire engine left, and so did the man on the scooter. Now she could watch more easily. But she hated to look. There was almost nothing left. A huge smouldering heap. The firemen still there were spraying their hoses on dying flames. Sickened, she turned away and slipped carefully, quietly, back to the house in the cemetery.

She made her way up to the bed in the back room slowly and heavily. She did not stop at Benjamin. There was no way she could repeat what she had seen. The whole thing was too fresh, too new, too awful to think about. Yet she could not get it out of her mind. Every time she closed her eyes, the flames were there. And the question. What did she do now? Her secret life was ended, unless she stayed forever in the cemetery. And that she did not intend to do, not yet.

A foster home? Was that the only answer? Or would her mother come back and find them another place to live? Could she depend on her mother now, when there was no house? Was there some place a girl alone could run to, could find a way to live alone?

She turned the problem over and over in her mind until finally she was so tired she went to sleep and didn't even dream. But it was a restless sleep even so. Underneath, her mind churned and boiled, and nothing would settle. She woke and slept, woke and slept, swirled through flame and cold and came to no answer.

It was late when she woke that morning, later than usual. And she knew the instant she was fully awake that a decision had to be made then. She couldn't put it off. But what choices did she have? She quickly laid out all the possibilities; there weren't many. And then out of the mists in her mind, the answer came: the only thing she could do. It was doing what she had to do, but doing it in a way that would work for her, that would make it possible for her to do it.

In half an hour she was ready to go. She had dressed, and put a few extra clothes and all her books into her book bag and shopping bag. The bags were heavy, but that didn't matter. She didn't have far to go. The bedding she would leave and the food and even some of her clothes. That wouldn't matter either.

She walked downstairs slowly. This was a good place. She wished she could stay here. But she knew she couldn't. Her food would run out. She had very little money. And she couldn't stay alone, anyway.

She placed her hand on Benjamin, whose glow had faded a good bit since yesterday.

"I'm here, and I'm going," she said. Briefly she described what had happened in the night.

"I thought I was going to run away," she said. "Even though you can't take me where you are, I thought there had to be some place I could go. But it wouldn't work."

"No, it wouldn't work," Benjamin echoed, almost as he had the first day he talked. Only last Thursday. It seemed like such a long time ago. "You won't stay in this house?"

"No, I can't. It wouldn't work. And with the house burning, if I went out for anything, people would ask questions. That's the worst: Whatever I do, people will ask questions, and what will I say? No, first I'll go to Mr. Simon. Tell him everything—except about you. He wouldn't understand that. I think he'll help me work something out, something not too bad."

"May it be as you want it, Lucinda. We wish you good. And we thank you."

She rubbed Benjamin's head casually. He still tingled. "I guess you'll be gone when I get back—if I ever do get back. Don't forget me," she said.

"No, we are not likely to forget. You have made your galaxy, your Earth at least, live for us in a way we could never have expected. Thank you for that, Lucinda. Thank you from all of us who have been Benjamin to you."

138 ≈

"You're welcome. Oh, you're very welcome," she said softly.

She picked up her bag and slipped out the door. It was after nine o,clock. Mr. Simon would be at his gate. There was no hurry. But it was time to go.

≈ ≈ ≈ ≈ ≈ ≈ ≈ ≈ ≈ ≈ ≈ ≈ ≈ ≈ ≈ ≈ ≈ ≈ ≈ **11**

LUCINDA moved through the bushes that lay between the fence and the path with the quietness born of her week of hiding. She really didn't have to hide anymore. If someone should find her, it wouldn't make much difference in the end. Yet she wanted to control things as long as she could. That meant telling Mr. Simon first, because she felt she owed it to him and because she believed he would be kind. After that she didn't know what would happen. That she couldn't control. Yet good or bad, she would face it. If she could live alone for a week in a cemetery and talk to someone from another galaxy, surely she could do whatever else she had to do.

She almost laughed as she thought how carefully she had packed her homework and books into her bag.

She had her science paper and part of her cemetery paper, carefully written. Yet she might never go back to her old school. She had no place to live here anymore, so how could she?

Near the gate, in sight of it but not quite there, she settled for a last time under a bush, to review what she was going to tell Mr. Simon and to pick her moment to approach him. She wanted to go there when she was sure he was alone.

She could see the gatehouse and realized that there was someone with him now, a workman it looked like. They were deep in conversation and looked upset. Was there still a flood? Had the dam broken?

When the man finally went away, she knew the moment had come. She pulled her courage together, got up, and walked toward the gatehouse.

She was unprepared for the look on Mr. Simon's face. It was one of shock. Opening the door, she said, "Mr. Simon, is something the matter? Are you sick?"

He sat down quickly and put his head in his hands. "I know they said there was no one in the house. But somehow I was sure they were wrong, that you were dead. But you weren't there!"

"No, I wasn't there. I was here. That's what I've come to talk to you about. I had to go to somebody. And you're the one I want to tell."

He looked up and nodded. "You told me about that gang. I worried about you. Thought maybe those punks had done something."

"No, they never caught me."

"I'd better call someone. Tell them you're here."

"No, wait. Not yet. Let me tell you all of it first, please."

"Well, if that's the way you want it. But there must be people worrying about you. Where's your mother?"

Lucinda sat down and began her story. She told him all she could. From the very beginning. From the time Joel left and even before, to make him understand.

"I didn't want you to know," she said finally. "Not that I was staying here. And at first I came to talk to you because I had to know how much chance there was of my being found. But after the first day, I came because I wanted to—because I liked to talk to you and I liked to see the cemetery. It's something from another time, isn't it, Mr. Simon? When people were different and things were easier."

Mr. Simon just sat for a moment, looking at her. She hoped he wasn't mad.

"You don't blame me for what I did?" she said finally. "Do you think it's awful that I hid in the caretaker's house?"

"I don't think it's awful that you hid there. I think it's awful that you had to hide there," he said. "Seems like you showed good sense. More than I can say for them others. I was just thinking what to do now. What do you want to do?"

For the first time Lucinda really had to think about what ought to come next. From what Mr. Simon had said earlier, it sounded as if the fire had been on the radio or in the newspapers. She hadn't thought about that. Cherry and Joel, and her mother, if she was near, would be worried.

"The only person in my family that I can get to by phone is my sister Cherry," she said. "I guess we should call Cherry."

"That makes sense," he said. "You have her phone number?"

"Yes, somewhere in here." She tugged at her bag and went through her things. The phone number should be in the little change purse with the money she had left. Yes, there it was.

She pulled it out and gave it to Mr. Simon. He turned to his phone and dialed the number. She waited and so did he, both listening to the sound of ringing at the other end. The ringing stopped, and Lucinda could hear a voice.

"Hello," said Mr. Simon. "Is Cherry Gratz there?"

There was a pause as the voice spoke.

"No, I'm not from a newspaper. You're Mrs. Rice, right? Well, my name is John Simon. I'm the gate-keeper at the cemetery across from the house where Cherry's mother and sister lived. And I have Lucinda here with me at the cemetery gatehouse. She came this morning and said she's been living in the cemetery. Some gang of kids took over the house. . . . Yes, here she is."

Lucinda reached out to take the phone. "Hello, Cherry?"

"Lucinda, we've been so worried. Joel called. We've been frantic! What happened?"

"I've been in the cemetery, you know, the house where I told you I went. Those kids came. Oh, Cherry, I can't tell you over the phone. Can I see you? What am I going to do now?" For the first time that morning, she felt as if she were going to cry.

She heard Cherry talk to Mrs. Rice.

"You're at the main gate, is that right? Not the one across from the house."

"Yes, the main gate."

"Mrs. Rice and I will be there as soon as we can drop the kids off someplace and drive over. You just stay there. And Mrs. Rice says don't get in touch with anyone else until we get there. It will be all right for you to stay there, won't it?"

"Can I stay here until they come, Mr. Simon?" she asked, turning to him.

"Sure thing. Long as you want. No one will bother us."

"Yes, it's okay," she said to Cherry.

"All right. We'll be there as soon as we can."

Lucinda turned from the phone, feeling a strange sense of freedom. Someone else was going to help. And it felt awfully good. Yet, there had been something good in doing things for herself, too, in making her own decisions. At least she knew she could, if she had to again.

"How long will it take 'em?" Mr. Simon asked.

"A half hour, maybe an hour. Depends on what

they do with the two little kids, the ones that aren't in school. And then there's the traffic."

"I guess there won't be anyone coming along here in that time. But I'll close the gate, just so we won't have any surprises. If someone does come, you just step into that lavatory, there. That way no one will see you before your sister comes and you decide what to do."

Lucinda nodded, and he stepped out to close the gate. When he came back, she said, "Mr. Simon, there must be lots more things I don't know about the cemetery. Maybe I won't ever get back here again. Could you tell me some more?" She thought that might keep her from worrying about what would happen once Cherry and Mrs. Rice got there.

"Well, I guess I could." He sat back and smiled thoughtfully. Then he began to tell her about some of the people who were buried there: women who had died of broken hearts, or when they were having children; men who had died in battle; even some people who had killed themselves. And now they lay all together in this peaceful place.

It was all so interesting Lucinda was surprised when she heard the bell at the gate and looked out to see Cherry peering in impatiently. Mr. Simon opened the gate, and Mrs. Rice drove in as Cherry came running up and threw her arms around Lucinda.

"Lucy, oh Lucy, I was so afraid. And I was so mad at myself. I felt I shouldn't have left you, should have done something about you, even if it meant giving up school and getting a full-time job so I could keep you with me. Somehow I never thought of the cemetery. I know you told me. But I didn't think of your being there last night. What happened to Mother? Where is she?"

"I don't know, Cherry. I don't know where she is."

"Come on inside," said Mr. Simon. "I don't have a crowd like this often, but I guess we'll all fit."

Once inside, Lucinda told Cherry and Mrs. Rice the whole story, just as she had told it to Mr. Simon. "I don't know where she went," she said at last of her mother. "And I didn't think I should call you, Cherry. Not before a week or ten days, since I promised. And besides, I was afraid you'd think I had to go to a foster home. And I didn't want that. You remember that Sally. I told you, you know, she was in my room. And she said they were awful, foster homes. Anything seemed better than that. But now our house is burned down. And I don't know what to do. Do you think Mother will come, find us another place?"

"I don't know, Love. I don't know. Maybe she will. But maybe she won't. Maybe she wanted ten days so she could get far away, get to a place where no one would look. She wanted to be rid of him—of all of us maybe." She paused sadly. "Oh, Lucinda, we've got to call Joel. I told you he called. And I didn't take time to call him back. He was so worried."

Mr. Simon insisted that they call at once. And Cherry and Lucinda both talked to Joel.

"Lucinda," he said, "you got to take care now. I had

146 ≈

your letter this morning after I talked to Cherry. I tried to call her, but she was gone. Next time you get in trouble, let me know sooner."

"I will, Joel," she said, the tears really starting down her cheeks for the first time. It was so nice not to be alone, to feel that people cared. Maybe things wouldn't be as bad as she had thought they would be.

"Lucinda," said Mrs. Rice in a businesslike voice. "We don't have to decide everything right away. Of course, you can come home with us for now. And we must call the police. And I want to call Mr. Rice. But don't try to plan too far ahead. We'll wait and see if your mother gets in touch with you, once people know you're alive and where you are. And if she does, or if she doesn't, things will have to be decided eventually. But don't worry; it can be done slowly. And whatever happens, I'll see that it's good and something that you'll like."

Again Lucinda felt relief. Maybe everything would work out. It was possible. Though she wouldn't have thought so before. And whatever else happened, she felt sure now that she would not lose Cherry or Joel. That was the thing that had worried her most.

"Shall I call the police?" Mrs. Rice asked.

Yes, Lucinda nodded. Best to get it over with.

There would be hard things. But in the end it would be all right. She was not alone. "We wish you good," Benjamin had said. And his wish was going to come true.

≈ ≈ ≈ ≈ ≈ ≈ ≈ ≈ ≈ ≈ ≈ ≈ ≈ ≈ ≈ ≈ ≈ ≈ # After

"YOU WENT back to the house that same day?" Joel asked.

"Yes, well, Mrs. Rice didn't want to. She thought I was tired and should go to her house and rest. But I wanted to when the newspaper people asked me. You know, I thought maybe I'd never see the place again. And I thought maybe I could tell Benjamin that things were going to be all right."

"You couldn't do that with them there, could you?"

"I thought maybe when no one was looking. But, oh Joel, he wasn't there. When we went into that house, I looked for Benjamin first thing, and the whole statue was gone. I don't know what those newspaper people thought, I was so quiet. Maybe that I was overcome by going back to the house. But it was Benjamin. There was no statue. I wondered if I'd been crazy all that time. But I remembered Mr. Simon had said he was there. And when I looked, there was a little hard ball of metal at the top of the pipe. So heavy and hard it had made the floor go down around it. Now, do you believe me, Joel? That couldn't have happened if it was just my imagination, could it?"

Joel laughed. "You always did get your stories straight, Lu. But I don't know what to think. It sounds so strange. It's so far out. And still, I can't imagine anyone making up a story like that. Besides, you never knew all that much about astronomy and such. And something happened to you in that house. You're not the same, Lu."

"What's not the same?"

"You're more curious. You know a lot more. Not just like things in school, but in a bigger way."

"You mean because I had to keep away from those kids, learn how to keep myself safe?"

"No, you always were a lot smarter than they were."

"I guess they *were* kind of dumb. I feel sorry for them now, I think. I only told on Tom Williams. I had to do that. But what happened after, well, that wasn't my fault. Tom Williams can't be mad at Dean anymore. Not when he told so much himself. But that's not what I want to talk about. Not about me. I want to know if you believe me about Benjamin. Do you think that galaxy did come here? And do you think other places, maybe, are trying to come here, too?"

"I don't know, Lu. I think I have to believe you.

But don't tell anyone else. They might not know you as well as I do."

"But you'll talk to me about it sometimes?"

"Sure, anytime. Now, what's it like here at the Burrows'? Do you like it?"

"It's great, not at all the way I thought a foster home would be. I like them, and I like the school and the kids. Did I tell you the teachers here gave me credit for those papers I wrote, and they sent copies to my old school, too? There's proof for you, Joel. Why would I do a paper on planets and galaxies if Benjamin wasn't true?"

"Okay, so I believe you. But Lu, you have to forget all that. We were lucky, both of us. And we have to work to keep it that way."

"Mama or Pa could come back. That could change things."

"No, I don't think they'll come back. The fire gave them both a way out. And you, too."

"I hope you're right. Though sometimes I think about Mama. She tried, Joel. She really did. And I love her. But I want to stay here. And I won't tell, Joel. Not about the other galaxy, I mean. I can't stop thinking about it sometimes, though. . . . And maybe someday I'll get in touch again—with them or someone else, even."

"Be practical, Lucinda. How can you do that?"

"Well, you take a cemetery with an electric fence. . . ."